FREDDY
and the IGNORMUS

. . . floating down silently . . . was a great white shape

FREDDY

and the

IGNORMUS

by WALTER R. BROOKS

Illustrated by Kurt Wiese

THE OVERLOOK PRESS
NEW YORK, NY

If you enjoyed this book, very likely you will be interested not only in the other Freddy books published in this series, but also in joining the *Friends of Freddy,* an organization of Freddy devotees.

We will be pleased to hear from any reader about our "Freddy" publishing program. You can easily contact us by logging on to either THE OVERLOOK PRESS website or the Freddy website.

The website addresses are as follows:

THE OVERLOOK PRESS
www.overlookpress.com

FREDDY
www.friendsoffreddy.org

We look forward to hearing from you soon.

This edition first published in paperback in the United States in 2011 by

The Overlook Press, Peter Mayer Publishers, Inc.
141 Wooster Street
New York, NY 10012
www.overlookpress.com
For bulk and special sales, please contact sales@overlookny.com

Dust jacket and endpaper artwork courtesy of the Lee Secrest collection and archive.

Library of Congress Cataloging-in-Publication Data

Brooks, Walter R., 1886-1958
Freddy and the Ignormus / Walter R. Brooks ; illustrated by Kurt Wiese.
p. cm.
Summary: Freddy the pig must summon all of his courage and detective skills when the chief suspect of a series of robberies on the Bean farm is a legendary beast from the Big Woods.
[1. Pigs—Fiction 2. Animals—Fiction 3. Mystery and detective stories]
I. Wiese, Kurt, 1887-1974, ill.
PZ7.B7994Fp 1998 [[Fic]—dc21 98-44-6

Manufactured in the United States of America

ISBN 978-1-59020-467-2

2 4 6 8 10 9 7 5 3 1

FREDDY
and the IGNORMUS

Chapter 1

If you went up the lane back of Mr. Bean's barn, you came to a little bridge that crossed a brook. And if you turned left and followed the brook upstream you came to the pond where Alice and Emma, the two ducks, lived, and then you went through a pasture and along beside the woods, and then you went right up into the woods themselves where everything was dim and cool, with only the chuckle of the running water and the occasional whistle of a pewee to break the stillness. And in a few minutes you came to a little pool. On one side it was steep and rocky and the trees wriggled their roots right down over the rocks into the water. But on the other side a smooth grassy bank sloped down to the water. Most days if you went up there you wouldn't find anybody but a frog, named Theodore, who lived there. But if you went up there on a good hot summer day, you would most likely find Freddy, the pig, reclining on the grassy bank, engaged in the composition of poetry.

If you are going to write poetry, you need two things. You need quiet and you need coolness. You can't have a lot of people talking to you, and you can't be all hot and sticky. Of course you also need paper and pencil. So Freddy always took these along, and he would lie on the bank and write a little, and then think a long time, and then write a little more. Sometimes he would do so much thinking and so little writing that Theodore thought he was asleep. But Freddy said no, he was just thinking very hard.

"But you don't snore when you're thinking," said Theodore.

"Sometimes I do," said Freddy. "Sometimes I do. When I'm thinking extremely hard, I snore like anything."

Theodore was very polite and so he didn't say any more.

Well one day Freddy was sitting by the pool trying to write a poem about ants. The poem was to be part of a book for animals—probably the first book for animals ever written. Of course most animals can't read, and so this was to be an alphabet book, to teach them their letters. At first he had planned to have the first chapter written with words that begin with A, and the next chapter to have nothing but words that begin with B, and so on. But he found that was too hard, so he decided to write just a sentence with all the words beginning with the same letter, and then write a poem about it. He had his first sentence: Ants Are Awfully Aggravating. And now he was thinking up the poem.

I guess he wasn't thinking very hard because he had his eyes open And pretty soon he saw something small and white come bounding down the path towards him. It looked almost like a tennis ball. But as it came closer he saw it was a rabbit.

"Here, here!" Freddy called irritably. "What's all the fuss about?"

The rabbit stopped short, gave a gasp, and then ran up to him.

"Oh, Mr. Freddy," he panted. "I—I'm so scared!"

There were a great many rabbits on the Bean farm, and when Freddy had been in the detective business he had hired them to investigate crimes and keep watch of suspicious characters and so on. He was at that time probably the largest rabbit employer in New York State. Most of them didn't have any names, and he had numbered them so that he could keep track of them.

"Well, well," said Freddy. "Let's see, now. You're Rabbit Number Twenty-One, aren't you? Yes, I remember. You helped me in several cases. Well, what are you scared of?"

So Number Twenty-One told him that he had been up in the Big Woods with his brother looking for watercress, of which rabbits are very fond. And something had scared him. He wasn't very clear about what it was, but that didn't surprise Freddy much. People who are scared are hardly ever very clear about what scared them. Freddy told Number Twenty-One that. "If you'd seen what it was that scared you," he said, "you probably wouldn't be scared any more. Because the more you know about a thing, the less scary it is. And if you know all about it, you find it isn't anything to be scared of at all. I suppose," he said, "you heard something rustling in the underbrush."

"Something rustled," said the rabbit, "and made a funny noise. And it followed us."

"Probably the wind," said Freddy. "Or a mouse. And I suppose your aunt has told you that you mustn't ever go into the Big Woods?"

"Yes," said the rabbit. "She says there's something there that eats rabbits. She says our great-grandfather went into the Big Woods once and was never heard of again. I guess we never paid much attention to what she said; we thought it was just a story she made up so we wouldn't go up there and get lost. But, my goodness, we'll never go there again."

"Well," said Freddy, "I don't know about your great-grandfather; he was before my time. But I do think it is very wrong of your aunt to try to frighten you with stories like that. Because there really isn't anything different about the Big Woods than there is about these woods we're in. There's a story about the Big Woods, of course. Nobody knows who they belong to now, but a long time ago they belonged to a man named Grimby. Mr. Grimby didn't like animals, and he wasn't very kind to them. He used to holler at animals and throw stones at them. Well, that went on for a long time, and all the birds and animals moved out of the Big Woods, and none of the farm animals ever went there.

"By and by Mr. Grimby moved away. But the animals thought he might come back, and so they still kept away from the woods. Of course he never did come back, and his old house, in the middle of the woods, is all falling to pieces. Lots of the animals even forgot why nobody went to the woods, and they began to make up stories to explain it. And if you listen to those stories, you'll get the idea that the Big Woods are a lot more dangerous than they were even when Mr. Grimby lived there. You'd think to hear some of these animals talk that there were lions and tigers and flying rhinoceroses up there."

"Have you ever been up to the Big Woods, Mr. Freddy?" Number Twenty-One asked.

"Why, yes," said Freddy, "I've been—well not exactly *in* the Big Woods, you understand, but I've been *by* there. And never saw nor heard a thing, not a thing. Nothing to be afraid of at all."

"I wouldn't be afraid to go up there with you," said the rabbit, "but when I'm alone—"

"When you're alone," said Freddy firmly, "and you hear or see something that scares you, the thing to do is to walk right up and find out what it is. Then see it's just a shadow, or a mouse, or a piece of paper fluttering in the wind, and you aren't scared any more."

"You're awfully brave, Mr. Freddy," said Twenty-One admiringly.

"Pooh!" said Freddy. "No, I'm not. No braver than any other pig. But that's just common sense."

"I suppose it is," said the rabbit. "But—oh, dear—I wish you'd walk up to the Big Woods with me, so I could see how it works. If I could see how you do it just once, why maybe the next time, when I'm alone, I'd be all right."

But Freddy said no, he was much too busy. "I've got this poem to finish today. You see, Twenty-One," he said importantly, "I'm writing a Book." He said it like that, with a capital letter, and I don't know that you can blame him, for there are very few books in the world the authors of which are pigs.

So Twenty-One thanked him for his advice and hopped off home, and Freddy was just settling down to work again when Theodore crawled out on the bank.

Theodore was a hermit. He liked to be

alone, and he was perfectly happy living all by himself in the pool in the woods. He had a fine bass voice and sometimes when the animals on the Bean farm were giving an entertainment they would ask him to sing. But he always refused. He said he'd be so nervous if he got up in front of all those animals that he wouldn't be able to sing a note. He liked to sing when he was all alone in the pool, the way some people like to sing in the bathtub. And on still nights his voice could be heard booming out over the countryside, and the animals would gather in the barnyard to listen. Even Charles, the rooster, who rather fancied himself as a singer, said that Theodore had one of the finest voices he had ever heard.

Theodore was handsome for a frog. At least, other frogs said he was, though as Mrs. Wiggins, the cow, said, he could be a whole lot handsomer than the whole frog tribe and still be pretty near the homeliest critter under the sun. And after all if your face is green, and you have a huge mouth, and bulging eyes, and nothing much in the way of a nose, you have to admit yourself that you're pretty homely. But Theodore had something better than good looks; he had style. His skin was bright green with black markings and fitted him perfectly, and when he jumped or swam he was so strong and graceful that you just had to watch him, and you forgot all about his homeliness.

"Hi, F-Freddy," said Theodore. "I hope you'll exc-cuse me, b-b-but I was just under the b-bank and c-c-couldn't help hearing you. B-but why didn't you go up to the bub-bub, I mean Big Woods with the poor little chap?" Theodore stammered a good deal. But the funny thing was that when he sang, he never stammered at all.

"Good gracious!" said Freddy. "If I had to go take care of every rabbit that got scared on this farm, I'd never get anything done. Do you realize how many rabbits get scared every day on a place this size? Anyway, Twenty-One is old enough to un-scare himself without my help."

"Mum, maybe that's true," said Theodore, "but I kind of f-figured maybe you thought if you went up there you'd have to un-scare yourself as well as him."

"Good gracious!" said Freddy.

"Pooh!" said Freddy. "What of? There's nothing there."

"Well, t-that's just what you said he was scared of—nothing. And I thought m-maybe you'd be scared of it too. Let's go up to the Big Woods, Freddy. I've been hearing stories about it ever since I was a tut-tut, I mean tadpole, but I've never been near the place. I bet you haven't either."

"No," said Freddy, "and don't want to."

"I c-can't understand you, Freddy," said Theodore. "A great t-traveler like you that's been to Florida and the North Pole and all those places. And here's a place only a mile away you've never been to. You weren't afraid to g-go to F-Florida—"

"I'm *not* afraid, I tell you," said Freddy. "I just can't take the time. Here's my book only part done—"

"Part done! " exclaimed Theodore. "You've been working on it a week, and all you've got is 'Ants Are Awfully Aggravating.' Four words! If you take today off you'll only m-miss writing about half of one word."

"That just isn't so," said the pig crossly. "You don't understand about writing poetry, Theodore. You have to think out an awful lot in your head before you put anything down on paper. For instance, I've already got the first line of the ant poem. 'The busy ant works hard all day.' Now I've got to get a rhyme for 'day'."

"Stay, hay, play—that isn't so hard," said the frog. "Look, if I give you a second line will you walk up to the Big Woods?"

"But you're not a poet," said Freddy. "How could you give me a second line?"

"The busy ant works hard all day," said Theodore, "and never stops to rest or p-play. There's your second line. I may not be a pup-pup-pup, I mean poet, but I can write poetry."

"Why, that's not bad," said Freddy. "Not bad at all."

"B-bad!" exclaimed the frog.

"Well, I mean—you could learn to write poetry all right. In time, of course. Yes, I think you might learn."

"Oh, d-don't b-be so high and m-m-mighty," said Theodore disgustedly. He always stuttered worse when he was excited. "Just because I'm a ſ-ſ-ſuſſ-ſ—"

"Fool?" suggested Freddy helpfully.

"No!" shouted Theodore. "I mean, fuf-fuf — Oh, gosh, what's the use!" And he turned around and dove into the pool.

"Well, dear me," said Freddy. He looked at the widening circle of ripples where Theodore had disappeared. "It was really a good enough line, at that. I shouldn't have kidded him. And I suppose after all, I could have gone up to the Big Woods with him. I *would* sort of like to see them."

"O K," said Theodore, hopping out on the bank again. "Let's g-go."

Freddy stared. "I thought you were in the water."

"No, I swum up under the b-bank again. You talk to yourself a lot, Freddy. I thought you'd pup-pup, I mean probably make some remarks."

"Oh, all right," said the pig resignedly. He tucked his paper and pencil under a stone, and they set out.

Chapter 2

If you follow along up the brook that runs through Mr. Bean's woods, pretty soon you come to a dirt road that is the boundary of the Bean property. The Big Woods are really a continuation of the Bean Woods on the other side of the road. But as soon as you cross the road into them you feel a difference. No thrushes or pewees sing in the Big Woods; there are none of the rustlings and patterings that tell you of little animals going about their daily business. Except for the chatter of the brook, everything is very still.

Freddy and Theodore went more and more slowly as they approached the road. Freddy's jog trot slowed to a walk, and Theodore's long jumps became short hops that even the smallest grasshopper would have been ashamed of. They crossed the road. And under the shadow of the trees on the other side they stopped.

"Well, this is The Big Woods," said Theodore.

"The Big Woods," said Freddy, looking around. "The Big Woods. Well, well." And after a minute he said: "I don't know how you feel, but I'm sort of tired. Long walk, hot day, and so on. I think I'll rest a little." And he sat down at the edge of the road.

Theodore sat down beside him, and they talked for a little while about the weather, and politics, and the coming-out party Charles, the rooster, had given for his youngest daughter, and about everything but the Big Woods. And then Freddy got up.

"Well," he said, "shall we go back now?"

"Go back!" said the frog. "Why, we haven't been anywhere yet."

"We've been to the Big Woods," said Freddy; "And that's where we said we were going."

"We've been *to* them, but we haven't been *in* them," said Theodore. "You couldn't say you'd been to a show if you just went up and looked at the outside of the theatre, could you? Look, Freddy, we ought to explore 'em as long as we're here. You're so bub-bub, I mean brave, I thought you'd plunge right into their very depths."

Freddy shook his head. "I don't pretend to be brave," he said modestly.

"Well, you're not a c-coward, are you?"

"Why no; I don't think I'm exactly a coward, Theodore."

"You've got to be either one thing or the other," said the frog. "If you're not brave, you're a coward, but if you're not a coward, then you're brave. You can't be both."

"O K, then I'm brave," said Freddy. "And where does that get us?"

"It ought to g-get us into the woods," replied Theodore.

"See here," said Freddy. "Let's just admit that we aren't either of us very brave, and go on back to the pool and be comfortable. Eh?"

But Theodore said no. "I'm not going to come all the way up here for nothing," he said. "I'm going to prove one thing anyway." He gathered his hind legs under him and made a long jump that carried him several yards into the woods. "I'm *that* much braver than you, Freddy."

Freddy got up. He looked into the dark shadows under the trees. "Oh, dear," he thought. And then he thought: "I can't let a frog get the best of me. I may be only a pig, but I've got some pride." And he marched into the woods.

Of course Theodore knew all about Freddy's career as a detective, and an explorer, and he had always thought of him as one of the most courageous animals alive. And when he discovered that he was just about as courageous himself, it went to his head and he took another jump. For he thought: "My goodness, if I can prove that I am braver than Freddy, I will get a big reputation and be invited to b-banquets and even maybe get my name in the pup-pup, I mean paper." (You will notice that he had got so used to hearing himself stutter that he even stuttered when he thought.)

But Freddy was not to be outdone. His reputation was at stake, and so he dashed after Theodore. And Theodore jumped again.

So pretty soon it became a race to see who could get farther into the Big Woods and prove himself the braver of the two. They tore on through bushes and over logs and stones and then all at once were stopped short by a thicket of briars and witch-hopple that it was impossible to push through. So they stood for a minute panting and looking at each other.

"My goodness, weren't we silly!" said Freddy.

"Yes," said Theodore. "My, isn't it still!"

"Too still," said Freddy. "The way it is before a thunderstorm. And every minute you expect it to go flash-bang! And yet you can't see anything."

He looked around. "The trouble with woods is, you can't see anything but trees."

"I'd rather not see anything else," said the frog. They were both speaking in undertones. And suddenly Theodore jumped straight up in the air.

"Wow!" he yelled. "What's that?"

Freddy jumped too, though not so high. "Don't *do* that!" he said crossly, as Theodore turned to look intently at the place where he had been standing a second before.

"Sorry," said the frog. "I d-didn't realize I was standing on an ant hill. One of 'em walked across my fuf-fuf, I mean foot."

"Let's get out of here," said the pig. "Oh, look! Did—did you see something move down behind that big hemlock? I don't mind telling you, Theodore, that I'm scared."

"You don't have to tell me," said the frog. "Your tail's come uncurled. Well, I'm scared too. C-come on."

If the race into the woods had been to decide which of them was the braver, the race out was to decide which was the scareder. And it too was a tie. They both reached the road at the same moment. And almost fell over a large grey rat who was plodding along the middle of it.

"Simon!" exclaimed Freddy. "What are you doing here? See here, you're not living in the neighborhood again, are you?" And he frowned, or at least tried to, for it is pretty hard to frown if you haven't any eyebrows.

The rat, who had looked startled to see Freddy, recovered himself and smiled an oily smile.

"My old friend, Freddy!" he said. "Dear, dear; what a pleasure to be sure! And how are all those other funny animals? And the good Beans?"

"It's no pleasure to me," said Freddy shortly. "And I may say that the other animals, and the good Beans, are quite ready to chase you out of the county again, as they did before, if they catch you up to any of your old thieving tricks."

Simon's long yellow teeth gleamed wickedly under his twitching whiskers. "Sticks and stones may break my bones, Freddy," he said, "but hard words cannot hurt me. You always were a big talker, but I can't remember that you ever did much." He snickered. "Remember up in the barn that night when you broke your tooth on the toy locomotive?" He turned to Theodore. "Freddy thought it was me he had hold of. Snapped one of his beautiful white teeth right off. We made up a song about it:

> *Freddy the sleuth,*
> *He busted a tooth—*

"That'll do for you, Simon," said the pig angrily. "What are you doing here? I thought you'd left the country."

"I don't see that it's any of your business, pig," said the rat. "This is a public road. I've got as good a right here as you. But I don't mind telling you. I've been visiting my relatives out in Iowa. That's a great place, Freddy. Lots of pigs in Iowa. But they don't make poetry.

"Dear, dear, what a pleasure!"

No, no. Out in Iowa the pigs make pork. Pork, not poetry, Freddy. You ought to take a little trip out there. Hey, quit!" he squealed, as Freddy made a sudden rush for him.

But Freddy was too exhausted by his gallop through the woods to chase Simon very far. He gave up, and the rat, who had dived into the ditch, climbed back on the road. "Smarty!" he grinned.

"All right, Simon," said Freddy. "I've warned you."

"Why, so you have, pig," replied the rat. "So it's only fair that I should warn you in turn. I judge by the speed with which you came out of the Big Woods, that something was after you. A bit foolhardy to venture in there, weren't you? When I lived in this neighborhood, I found out some things about the Big Woods that you smart farm animals don't know. I don't like you, Freddy, as you may have gathered, but on the other hand, I wouldn't want to see you eaten up. And so I'm warning you—don't go into the Big Woods again. The next time he'll get you."

"He?" said Theodore. "Who?"

Simon lowered his voice. "Come over here," he said, crossing to the Beans' side of the road. "He's probably listening now, and it's just as well if he doesn't hear us talking about him. I can't tell you much about him, except his name, and that he's very big and ferocious, and walks very, very quietly. And then, from be hind a tree—pounce! Snip-snap! No more Freddy!"

"Nonsense!" said Freddy. "There's nothing in there. We didn't see anything. We-we were just having a race."

"That's what I gathered," said the rat with a snicker. "You were racing him, and you won— this time. Well, I shan't be able to say, 'I told you so,' because when the Ignormus gets you, there won't be any Freddy to say it to."

"The what?" asked Theodore.

"The Ignormus," said Simon. "Well, now I've warned you. Good-bye, gentlemen."

"I don't like the s-sound of that much," said Theodore when Simon had gone off down the road.

"Pshaw," said Freddy, "don't let that upset you. Simon is the worst liar in three counties. If he tells you anything, you can be pretty sure that the truth is something different. Anyway, Theodore, we have explored the Big Woods."

"And got g-good and scared," said the frog. "I guess I was wrong to say that you couldn't be brave and cowardly at the same tut-tut, I mean time. Because we were brave too, to go in at all."

"I guess," said Freddy, "that all brave deeds are like that. Only later, when the people who did them tell about them, they forget the cowardly part. Maybe it would be just as well if we did the same thing. After all, we *did* go in.— But, my goodness, I must get down to the farm and tell the animals that Simon and his gang are back in the country again. We'll have to do something about that. Come along, Theodore."

Chapter 3

Jinx, the cat, had company. His sister, Minx, had come to pay him a visit. All the animals had been very anxious to meet her, for Jinx had talked about her a good deal, and if what he said was so, she was the smartest animal that ever lived. According to Jinx, she was almost as smart as he was. She had belonged for several years to a purser on a steamship and she had been to Europe and to South America and to a lot of countries that the animals had never even-heard of.

That afternoon Mrs. Wiggins, the cow, and her two sisters, Mrs. Wogus and Mrs. Wurzburger, had given a party for Minx in the cow barn. It had been a nice party, for Mrs. Bean had baked a cake for it, and the cows had been able to use the new paper napkins the Beans had given them for Christmas. They were very handsome napkins; Some were blue and some were pink, and they all had a big W in one corner, surrounded with a wreath of flowers. The W was nice, because it stood for all three of their names.

But Minx hadn't made as big a hit at the party as Jinx hoped she would. The animals liked her all right, but they agreed that she was pretty irritating. For there wasn't anything you could mention that she didn't know all about, and if you'd seen a big something, she'd seen a bigger on her travels. And she'd really quite hurt Mrs. Wiggins' feelings. For when the napkins were brought out, everybody praised them and said how handsome they were, and Minx said they were indeed the most superior paper napkins she had ever seen. But she didn't have the sense to leave it at that. She went on to say that on the last cruise she had taken, the napkins on the boat were pure linen, with the name of the ship woven right in them.

Even Jinx got a little mad at this, and he said: "Oh, what's the matter with you, Sis? You'll wipe your whiskers on these paper napkins, and like it."

So Minx saw what she had done, and she apologized very prettily. But a minute later, when Alice, one of the ducks, began telling how she had once ridden on a baby elephant at the circus, Minx interrupted before Alice had finished to tell how one time in Africa, *she* had taken a long trip through the jungle on the back of an elephant, eight feet high.

When the cake had all been eaten up, the animals went out to try the swing that Mr. Bean had just put up for them on the apple tree by the side of the cow barn. A lot of Mr. Bean's neighbors laughed at him for doing things like that for his animals. They said it was silly for a farmer to put muslin curtains in the windows of the cow barn, and electric lights and a revolving door in the henhouse, and to encourage his animals to play games, and learn to read, and take vacations. But Mr. Bean didn't bother to argue. When people said things like that to him, he just grunted and said: "Whose animals are they?" They didn't get much satisfaction out of him.

None of the animals had tried the swing yet, and at first they all stood around and looked at it and said: "You try it, Robert." "Why don't you get in it, Alice?" "Go on, Jinx, you show 'em." But nobody got in, until at last Charles, the rooster, said he'd take a swing if Mrs. Wiggins would push him.

Charles tried to make out that he was pretty brave to be the first one, but of course he had wings, and if he fell out, all he'd have to do was spread his wings and fly down to the ground. He stood on the seat and Mrs. Wiggins pushed him—back and forth, back and forth, higher and higher. Charles was so excited that he crowed all the time, and Mrs. Bean heard him and came to the kitchen door to see what was going on. "My land," she said, "that looks like fun. I haven't done that since I was twelve years old." And she sat down to watch.

Charles liked swinging so much that they had a hard time getting him to give the other animals a chance at it. But finally he got down, and Jinx jumped on the seat. So Mrs. Wiggins swung him, and she swung Robert and Georgie, the two dogs, and Henrietta, Charles's wife, and Minx—who said that in South America they used to swing on the long trailing creepers that hung from the trees, a hundred feet long or more. And then Mrs. Wiggins said she guessed she'd try it herself if Hank, the old white horse, would swing her.

Mrs. Wiggins had some trouble getting into the swing, partly because she was so big, and partly because she got to laughing. But Robert and Georgie held the seat and she got in finally, and Hank started to push her. Everybody thought she'd get scared when the swing began to go, but she didn't. "Land sakes, it's just like flying," she said. "Swing me higher, Hank." And then as the swing swooped down:

"Whee!" she yelled.

Well it certainly was quite a sight to see, a cow flying through the air and up among the green apple boughs—although of course Minx said she'd seen cows performing on a trapeze many times in Holland. But it came to a very sudden end. For just as Mrs. Wiggins was coming down on the highest swing yet, and had started to shout "Whee!" again, around the corner of the cowbarn dashed Freddy. He hadn't seen what was going on, and without knowing it he ran right across the path of the swing, and Mrs. Wiggins hit him squarely. Her hind legs shot under him and he was scooped up as a ball is scooped up by a golf club, and tossed right over the ring of animals who were looking on, into a very large and very thick and very prickly barberry bush.

Everybody said, "Oh, my goodness!" and ran over to the bush, and Minx began telling about a pig she knew in Mexico who had jumped into a hedge of prickly pear, which had *much* longer thorns than barberry and which—

. . . he was scooped up

"Oh, keep still, Sis," said Jinx. "Nobody cares about your old pig. We've got to see if Freddy's hurt."

And just then Freddy's head poked up out of the middle of the bush. He looked mad and scared and surprised and worried and determined, and so the animals knew he wasn't hurt, because if he had felt any pain he couldn't have had all those other feelings too. But Jinx asked him if he was hurt, because that is the natural thing to ask in such circumstances.

"No, I'm not hurt," said Freddy. "But somebody else is going to be, when I get out of here. Playing a trick like that on me! "

"Nobody played any trick," said Mrs. Wogus. "You got in my sister's way when she was swinging. And—oh, my goodness—that reminds me. Did anybody stop her?"

They all turned and looked. Sure enough, nobody had stopped the swing, and as Mrs. Wiggins didn't know how to stop it herself, there she was still swinging back and forth and trying, as she swooped up and down, to see what had happened to Freddy.

When they had stopped the swing and got Mrs. Wiggins out of it—and that wasn't an easy job either—they looked around for Freddy. But Freddy hadn't moved. His head was still sticking out of the bush, in the same place.

"For goodness sake," said Jinx, "are you going to stay there all night? You look like the last peach on the tree, with all those leaves around you. What are you doing—writing a poem?"

"I can't get out," said Freddy crossly. "Every time I move a thorn sticks into me in a new place. You might help me a little."

Jinx shook his head. "I don't know, Freddy," he said. "We'd have to tear the bush all apart, and you know how fond Mrs. Bean is of it. I guess you'll just have to stay there. If you just stay still it won't be so bad. We'll bring your meals to you."

"You wait till I get out of here, cat," said Freddy furiously. "I'll fix you."

"That's just it," said Jinx. "I guess I'll just have to wait. I guess—"

"Oh, come along, Jinx," said Mrs. Wiggins. "Let's get him out. You've had your fun." And she began pulling at the long thorny stems.

The other animals helped her, and so of course did Jinx. Freddy yelled a bit, but they got him out finally, and then looked him over carefully.

"If any of the scratches are very deep," said Alice, "you ought to have Mrs. Bean put iodine on them."

Freddy said quickly that they didn't hurt a bit.

"You ought to get a few more," said Jinx. "That kind of criss-cross marking looks well on your skin. I always say a pattern's prettier than just a plain color."

"I'll put some marks on you!" exclaimed Freddy, and went after the cat, who ran up the apple tree.

So then Mrs. Wiggins explained what had happened, and said how sorry she was, and showed Freddy the swing, and he got into it to try it. And he was just getting going good, with Hank to push him, when he suddenly remembered that he hadn't told them about Simon. "Oh, I meant to tell you," he called, and in his eagerness he let go of the ropes, and the swing swooped up and tossed him right back into the barberry bush again.

Jinx laughed until he almost fell out of the apple tree. "My goodness," he said, when Freddy's head appeared again in the middle of the bush, "you certainly are persistent! I suppose you're where the word pig-headed comes from. If you wanted to stay in that bush, why didn't you say so, and we wouldn't have got you out."

Some of the other animals seemed inclined to agree with the cat, for they had all got more or less scratched helping Freddy out the first time. But when Jinx came down from the tree and started tugging at the spiny branches, they went to work and got him out. "And now if you go back in there again," said Mrs. Wurzburger, who had pulled at a branch with her mouth and got some prickers in her tongue, "you can just stay there."

But Freddy had had enough. He thanked

the animals and trotted off home. It wasn't
until he was back in his study in the pigpen,
and had put some camphor ice on the scratches
to make them stop smarting, that it occurred
to him that he hadn't told them about Simon.
And what was even more important, he hadn't
told them that he had been in the Big Woods.

"I guess I'd better call a meeting tonight,"
he thought. "I'll get busy and write out my
petition and then prepare my speech."

Chapter 4

The summer that Mr. and Mrs. Bean went abroad, they left the animals in charge of the farm. And in order to run things properly, the animals formed the First Animal Republic and elected Mrs. Wiggins President. Of course after the Beans got back and took charge again, there was no special need for a government of this kind, but sometimes things came up that the animals didn't want to bother Mr. Bean with, and so they kept the F.A.R. as a going concern, with Mrs. Wiggins in office, and a small standing army of rabbits to run errands and so on. Besides, the animals were pretty proud of being citizens of the only republic of animals, by animals, and for animals in the world. It was, as Charles had said in one of his many speeches, an honor and a privilege which he, for one, would not lightly forego.

So when Freddy wanted to call a general meeting, he had first of all to send a petition to the President. So he wrote it out on the dusty old typewriter that he had in his study.

Hon. Mrs. Wiggins,
President, First Animal Republic,
Bean Farm, N. Y.

Your Excellency:
  It having come to my attention that a no-torious robber, to wit, one Simon, a rat, has been seen in this vicinity; and it being my firm conviction that the presence of said Simon is a danger and a menace to the peace of our beloved state; and it being further my hunch that said Simon is up to mischief: therefore I

*do most humbly petition Your Excellency to
call this same evening a general meeting of
citizens, to debate and take counsel upon such
measures as may be necessary to preserve the
peace and security of our glorious republic.*

(Signed) *Freddy*

When he had written this out, he went to
the door and called a passing sparrow, and
asked him to take it at once to Mrs. Wiggins.

Of course Freddy could just have gone over
to the cowbarn and said: "Simon's back. How
about a meeting tonight?" But affairs of state
are not conducted in such an offhand manner.
Mrs. Wiggins as a friend who had just knocked
him into a barberry bush, and Mrs. Wiggins as
President of the F.A.R. were two very different people. Freddy might, and probably
would, talk the matter over with her as between friends later, but now he was addressing
her as president of a sovereign state of which
he was a citizen. He had to put on a lot of
dignity, because if he didn't, none of the
others would either, and pretty soon when
Mrs. Wiggins gave an official order, nobody

would pay any attention to it.

As soon as Mrs. Wiggins got the petition, she sent for Jinx and Robert, and had them hoist the flag of the F.A.R. This was a good deal like the American flag, with two stars for Mr. and Mrs. Bean, and thirteen stripes, for the thirteen animals who had gone on that first historic trip to Florida. Usually it was only flown on holidays, like the Fourth of July, and Washington's and Lincoln's Birthdays, and May Third, which was the anniversary of the founding of the F.A.R. But when it was flown on any other day, it was a signal to all the animals that there was to be a general meeting that night.

When the flag was up, Mrs. Wiggins called out the standing army. Twenty-eight rabbits responded, and after putting them through a short drill, she sent them out into the woods and pastures, and along by the creek, to tell any animals who didn't notice that the flag was up, about the meeting.

When Freddy climbed up into the front seat of the old phaeton beside Mrs. Wiggins that night to address the meeting, the big barn was crowded to the doors.

Even Old Whibley, the owl, who never left the woods if he could help it, was there.

"Fellow citizens," said Freddy, "I have asked to have this meeting called because a grave danger threatens our state. It is a free state, and any animal or bird living within its boundaries, regardless of size, species, color or number of legs, is free to enjoy its privileges. Every animal and every bird has equal rights under the flag of the F.A.R."

At this point there was prolonged cheering, and when it had died down, Freddy went on. "Every animal but one. For I think you will agree with me that there is no place in a republic of free animals, for rats."

"Right, Freddy! Down with rats!" shouted a squirrel, and there was a general mutter of approval through the audience.

"It may be," said Freddy, "that there are good rats in the world. But our experience with them here has not been a happy one. You all know Simon; you know the trouble he has caused us in the past. You have all slept more peacefully in your beds since he was driven out of the country. But my friends—" Freddy paused impressively—"Simon has come back!"

After the excitement caused by this announcement had quieted down, Freddy started to tell his story. "I was coming back this afternoon from an exploring trip in the Big Woods," he began. But at once the whole audience was on its feet. "The Big Woods!" they shouted, and all began talking confusedly together and yelling questions at Freddy. Mrs. Wiggins had to pound on the dashboard repeatedly with her hoof to restore order.

"Fellow animals," she said, "this is as much of a surprise to me as it is to you. If anyone but Freddy came here with a story of having been into the Big Woods I'm afraid I wouldn't believe him. But you all know Freddy. My land, Freddy exaggerates some when he tells a story. I guess all poets do. But if he says he's been to the Big Woods, I guess he has. Let's all be quiet now and let him tell us about it."

So Freddy stood up again, very pink and

important, and told them the whole story. At least he told all but the part about how hard Theodore had to work to get him to go, and the part about his being so scared his tail uncurled, and the part about how hard they ran to get out again. And there were a few other little parts he didn't tell. There was quite a lot left of the story though—enough to make most of the animals feel that Freddy had been pretty brave. And after all he had been—and why shouldn't he get a little glory out of it? I don't see why.

But there were some who didn't believe the story, and one of them was Charles. At least he said he didn't, though perhaps he was only pretending, so that he would have an excuse for making a speech. Like most people who love to make speeches, he could talk for hours on any subject, whether he knew anything about it or not, and the things he said sounded fine until you thought about them, and then you realized that they didn't mean much of anything. So when the meeting was thrown open for discussion, he got up.

"Fellow citizens," he began, "we are gathered together here under the glorious banner of the F.A.R.; a banner, as you know, whose bright stripes and shining stars were flung to the breeze on that historic May 3d when we, as free animals, banded together in the name of liberty to form the first animal state on this continent. Long may they wave, my friends. Long may they flutter, above the humble cot of the lowliest rabbit, as above the palatial mansion of a Mr. Bean."

Old Whibley, the owl, who had been sitting with his eyes shut, suddenly gave a hoot of impatience. "Cut out the fireworks, rooster," he said. "This isn't the Fourth of July."

Charles, for once, looked a little confused. He had, as a matter of fact, got mixed up, and started by mistake on an oration which he had delivered the preceding July Fourth. But he recovered himself quickly.

" My venerable friend reminds me," he said, with a sour look at Old Whibley, "that this is no time for oratory. And he is right. There are

"There are matters of grave moment before this gathering."

matters of grave moment before this gathering. Leaving aside, for the nonce, the matter of Simon's reappearance—"

"What's a nonce, Charles?" called Jinx.

"Why, it's a—it's a—" Charles looked angrily at the cat. "Oh, let me alone, will you? I'm just trying to say that this story of Freddy's, about having been in the Big Woods, just isn't believable. It's—"

"You mean he's a liar?" said Jinx, and a bluejay laughed. "He may be a liar," he said, "but he isn't as big a liar as that."

"Listen, my friends," said Charles. "*You* know and *I* know that no animal has been to the Big Woods and returned alive in all the history of the Bean farm. Why not? Because there is something there. *Something!* And what is that something? You don't know and I don't know. The only animals who can answer that question are not here tonight, because—" He lowered his voice impressively— "because *they have been eaten up.*"

"That's right," whispered the audience. "Nobody has ever come back."

"Is it a lion with the head of an eagle?" Charles went on. "Or is it, as some old legends tell, a bird with the head of a lion? Is it a mysterious Something? Is its name, as Simon says, the Ignormus? No one knows."

"If you just got up to tell us that you don't know anything," said Old Whibley, opening one enormous yellow eye, "you can sit down again. We knew that before."

"Silence in the gallery!" said Charles crossly. "I am just trying to say that I think Freddy will have to give us some proof that he has been to the Big Woods. If old Hoot-and-Goggle up there will let me," he added with an angry look at the owl.

Old Whibley laughed. "Best thing you've said yet. Old Hoot-and-Goggle, eh? Not bad. Go ahead, then, old Scratch-and-Peck."

But Freddy interrupted. "Since I've been called a liar, " he said, " I think I have a right to protest. Charles wants more proof than just my word and Theodore's, does he? Well, all right. I'll go into the Big Woods with him any day he sets. I've been there before; I'm not afraid to go again."

There was prolonged applause at this bold speech, and all the animals looked at Charles. The rooster didn't look very brave. His tail feathers drooped and if there had been anything to crawl under, he would have crawled under it. But perched on the dashboard of the phaeton, he was completely surrounded. There was no escape.

He pulled himself together. "I have heard the challenge," he said, "and I reject it with the contempt which it deserves. Believe me, my friends, it takes more courage to do this, than to accept; to let you think that I am afraid, rather than to march boldly into the Big Woods, there to brave whatever perils it may hold. But I have a wife; I have twenty-six small children. What would happen to them, if in a moment of foolhardy bravado I were to be swallowed up forever in the shadow of those enormous trees? No, no, my friends. Alluring as the prospect of this adventure is, I must decline.

"And I ask you, what would it prove? Suppose we do come out again unharmed. Would my word be taken more quickly than Freddy's? Would you believe me, any more than you believe him?"

But a disturbance had begun at the back of the barn, and now it got louder. "Take Freddy up!" the animals shouted. "Either sit down, or go up to the Big Woods with Freddy." Charles began to look pretty worried.

Suddenly Henrietta, Charles's wife, jumped up beside him. She ruled the rooster with a claw of iron, and he was usually pretty scared of her, but when he got into trouble she always stood by him. "Listen, you animals," she said. "You're having a lot of fun with Charles, aren't you? Well, I don't deny he talks too much. But he isn't any coward. And he'll go to the Big Woods with Freddy. But on one condition. That is that one other animal among those present volunteers to go along. Well now, come along; who'll it be?"

But nobody answered. The animals all looked at the ground, and some of those who had been noisiest began to edge quietly towards the door.

"Come on," said Henrietta. "Who'll it be? You, Mrs. Wogus?"

"Land sakes, no," said the cow. "Wild horses wouldn't drag me into those woods."

"I guess you wouldn't find a wild horse to drag you, nor a tame one, either," said Hank. "No, you needn't look at me, Henrietta."

Henrietta pointed from one animal to another with her claw, but they all refused. Charles was beginning to perk up, when suddenly Little Weedly, Freddy's young cousin, stepped forward.

"I'll go," he said.

Henrietta looked surprised, and Charles said: "Oh dear me, that's very courageous of you, but I'm afraid you're much too young for such an expedition. Your mother would never consent."

"I'm old enough to vote," said Weedly. "I voted for Mrs. Wiggins at the last election. So I guess I'm old enough to go along with you and Cousin Frederick."

"Certainly you are," said Henrietta. "And

now let's settle on a time."

"How about—let me see," said Charles; "would a week from next Thursday be a good time? I can't say definitely without consulting my engagement book, but—"

I'll be your engagement book," said Henrietta, "and suppose we say tomorrow morning at nine."

"All right with me," said Weedly, and Freddy said that suited him.

Charles didn't look very happy, but he was still on the dashboard of the phaeton, surrounded by an admiring audience, and a lot of things could happen before tomorrow at nine. So he cleared his throat and said: "Well, my friends—" But he didn't get any farther because Henrietta seized his wing and pulled him down. "You'll do your speechifying *after* you've been to the Big Woods, not before," she said. "Right now you're going home and get some sleep." And she hustled him out through the crowd.

"Well," said Mrs. Wiggins, "now that that's settled, suppose we get back to the business of the evening. Freddy has seen Simon, and I guess we can be pretty sure that the rest of his family aren't far away. Of course, he may just have been coming back from Iowa, as he said, and not be staying in this neighborhood at all. But we can't take any chances with rats. Has anyone seen any rats around?"

But no one had.

"In that case," said Mrs. Wiggins, "about all we can do is to keep a sharp watch. Jinx, it's your job to keep an eye on those sacks of corn upstairs, and the oat bin, and so on. I don't have to give you instructions as to what to do if you see Simon or any of his gang. Probably your sister Minx can be of some help there."

"When I was in Spain a few years ago," said Minx, "in the town where I was visiting, there was a rat named Pablo. He was very large and ferocious, and was known as the king of the rats—"

"And she knocked him out in the third round," put in Jinx hastily. "That'll do, Sis. This isn't a bragging party: this is business."

"Well, I don't know," said Mrs. Wiggins.

"I don't think you need to be rude to your sister, Jinx—"

"You don't know her," said Jinx. "She's like Charles in some ways: you just have to be rude to her, or go deaf. But excuse me, your Excellency; you were about to say?"

"My goodness," said Mrs. Wiggins, "what was I going to say? Oh, yes. Where's the standing army?"

"Here, your Excellency," piped a little voice, and the rabbits filed up and stood in a row in front of the phaeton.

So then Mrs. Wiggins gave them their instructions. Each rabbit was to patrol a section of fence, or a strip of road, bounding the farm, and keep an eye out for the rats. If any were seen, they were to run at once and report to her, or to Jinx. "And beyond that," she said, "I don't see what else there is to do, for the present. Has anyone any suggestions?" And as no one had, she said: "Then I think for the rest of the evening we might play games."

So checker boards and parchesi boards and tiddleywinks sets were brought out, and

some of the animals played these games, and
others chose up sides for a spelling bee, a form
of entertainment that had grown very popular
since so many of them had learned to read. At
the far end of the barn some of the older animals chose partners for square dances, which
they went through to the music of a small
radio which Mr. Bean had had put in the winter before when Hank had been confined to
his stall with the rheumatism.

But at ten o'clock sharp the party broke up.
For that was one thing Mr. Bean was particu-
lar about.

Chapter 5

Charles, the rooster, sat on the fence. In the east, the sun was just coming up, pushing a flock of little pink clouds in front of him. Charles took a deep breath and threw back his head as if he was about to crow; then he let the breath out again and shook his head dejectedly. "Oh, dear," he said. "Oh, dear."

He had perched on this rail so many mornings to crow that it was all worn smooth. "Thousands of mornings," he thought; "thousands of mornings it took to do that.

And never a one of them on which I did not look forward to the day with happy expectation. Never a one until today. Oh, dear."

The sun's rim was now a tiny gold line above the horizon. It was Charles's job to get everybody on the farm out of bed before the sun was high enough to cast a shadow. There were no shadows yet, but in a minute or two there would be. Already a sort of ghost of a shadow stretched towards him from every tree and bush and fence between him and the sun. Well, he had to crow; better get it over with. So he took another deep breath and crowed.

It was a pretty poor crow,—weak and husky, and hardly loud enough to wake up a mosquito. And Henrietta stuck her head out of the henhouse door.

"What's the matter with you, Charles?" she said. "Give! Give! You sound like a sick katydid."

"Well, I-I don't feel very well this morning," said Charles. "Maybe it's this weather. I've had several sharp twinges in my second joint. I think perhaps I'd better go back to bed."

"I think perhaps you'd better not try to,"

said Henrietta. "Look at all those shadows, and you've only crowed once. You know what happens to roosters who don't stick to their jobs. They get fricasseed."

"I don't know but I'd just as soon be," Charles mumbled. But as Henrietta came out of the henhouse and started towards him with fire in her eye, he crowed several times more.

"That's better," said the hen.

"Well, *now* can I go back to bed?" said Charles. "I don't know what it is, but really, I just ache all over."

But Henrietta had heard this before. Charles always ached all over and had to take to his bed when he had to do something he didn't want to. "You'll just have to ache, then," she said. "Because you don't come back into this henhouse until you've been up to the Big Woods."

Charles looked at the long shadows on the grass, and then he thought of the much deeper and darker shadows in the Big Woods, and he shivered. "Oh, dear," he said miserably.

Henrietta took pity on him. "There's one thing you want to remember," she said.

"Freddy's just as scared of the woods as you are. If he goes more than two feet into them, I miss *my* guess. And you don't have to go any farther in than he does, so there isn't much to worry about. Only, make no mistake about it," she said: "you're *going.*"

Charles didn't ache so much when he thought that Freddy was scared too, and he was able to eat a good breakfast. He was almost cheerful when Weedly came for him, and he went along without protesting, although he cast several longing looks back at the safe and comfortable henhouse as they started up along the brook.

"Better hurry," said Weedly. "I'm afraid I'm a little late. Freddy said he'd meet us at the second big maple you come to as you go through Mr. Bean's woods."

When they passed the duck pond, Alice and Emma came waddling up. "You're really going, then?" said Alice. "I do think you're dreadfully brave."

Charles stuck out his chest. "Pooh!" he said. "A little stroll in the woods—what's that to be scared of?"

"That's the way our Uncle Wesley used to talk," said Emma. "Do you remember, sister? He just wasn't afraid of anything."

"He loved danger," said Alice. "He would have walked right up to a lion and quacked in his face. I've often thought that when he disappeared, something like that must have happened. He was just *too* fearless."

Charles would have liked to stay and be praised some more, but they were late and Weedly hurried him along. They went into the woods and at the second big tree they came to Weedly stopped.

"This doesn't look like a maple tree to me," said Charles.

"It's the second big one," said Weedly. "A tree's a tree. Why is a maple tree any different than any other?"

"My goodness, you're ignorant!" said the rooster. "A maple tree is as different from an elm tree as a—a raspberry bush is from a strawberry bush."

"Strawberries don't grow on bushes," said Weedly. "I know *that* much."

"Well, you know what I mean. And in my opinion this is *not* a maple. We must go on farther."

As they went on, Charles explained what a maple was like. He was always ready to explain anything, and this is a nice characteristic if you know what you're talking about. Charles usually didn't. And so the tree he finally chose to wait under for Freddy was a large beech, nearly quarter of a mile beyond the tree Freddy had meant.

So there they were in the woods, Freddy under his maple, and Charles and Weedly under the beech. It got to be nine o'clock, and it got to be half-past, and it got to be ten. Charles got more and more impatient.

"I can't stay here all day," he said. "Freddy's backed out on us. I'm going home."

"Cousin Frederick wouldn't do such a thing!" said Weedly indignantly. "You can go home if you want to, but I'm going on to the Big Woods. We've made a mistake in the meeting place probably."

"This heart has never quailed before peril."

"He's got to writing his poetry," said Charles. "That's what's happened, and he's forgotten all about us. Not that I blame him. There's no point in this expedition anyway. Come along, Weedly."

"No," said the pig firmly. "I said I'd go, and I'm going. If you're afraid, go on home."

"Afraid!" said Charles. "Pooh! Little do you know me, pig, if you think the heart that beats in this bosom—" and he whacked his chest with his claw—"has ever known fear. No, no, my young friend, this roosterly heart has never quailed before peril. But since Freddy is not here, I ask myself—what is to be gained? What will it prove?"

But Weedly was not listening. He had started on up through the woods. "I'll tell 'em you didn't want to go," he called back over his shoulder. And Charles, after a moment of hesitation, gave a sigh and followed.

Just about this time Freddy got tired of waiting, too. He had been sitting under his tree, putting the finishing touches on the A verse of his alphabet book. It went like this:

ANTS, ALTHOUGH ADMIRABLE, ARE
AWFULLY AGGRAVATING

The busy ant works hard all day
And never stops to rest or play.
He carries things ten times his size,
And never grumbles, whines or cries.
And even climbing flower stalks,
He always runs, he never walks.
He loves his work, he never tires,
And never puffs, pants or perspires.

Yet though I praise his boundless vim
I am not really fond of him.

Freddy was pretty pleased with the verse, and I think he had a right to be. But where were Charles and Weedly? "Guess they couldn't get Charles started," he said to himself. "Well, that lets me out." He started to go back home, and then he stopped. "Ho," he said, "if Charles didn't go, and if I don't go either, everybody will say we fixed it up between us not to go. They'll say we agreed to stay home, because we were scared. But if I go and Charles doesn't, then it will be Charles who will have to do the explaining. Goodness knows I don't want to, but after all, nothing happened to me before." And he turned around and went on.

When he got to the road that separated Mr. Bean's woods from the Big Woods, he hesitated a minute, and then he crossed it and dove into the shadow of the trees on the other side. He didn't know that about two minutes earlier Weedly and Charles had crossed it in almost the same place. "There's no point," he said to himself, "in going very far in. It's all alike; it's all just—woods. So it's just as brave to be in it out here at the edge as it would be to go right into the middle.

"And anyway," he said, "there isn't anything here."

Freddy knew that nothing Simon said was to be relied on, and he didn't believe that any such creature as the Ignormus existed. At least he didn't believe it when he was sitting at home in his comfortable study. But up here in the queer gloomy silence of the Big Woods it was easy to believe almost anything. He began to wonder what the Ignormus could be like. It would be big, and it would be ferocious, he thought, and it would have sharp claws and narrow yellow eyes. The longer he imagined it, the more awful it got. He added horns and tails and wings until he had an animal beside which a Bengal tiger would look as gentle and harmless as a pussy cat. And of course he got more and more scared. He tiptoed along, being very careful to make as little noise and to keep as well hid as possible, for undoubtedly the Ignormus, besides being very sharp of hearing, would have a very short temper. And he was thinking that perhaps he had gone far enough for one day when a little distance off to the right a twig snapped sharply.

Now twigs don't snap all by themselves. They snap when somebody steps on them. And if you're in woods where there are certainly no other animals, but where there *may* be Ignormuses, then the chances are that an Ignormus is not far away. At least that's how

Freddy figured it out. He dropped flat on the ground—or at least as flat as a rather fat pig could get—and lay there trembling. How was he to know that it was his Cousin Weedly who had stepped on that twig—and who was now cowering with Charles behind a bush not twenty yards away?

For quite a while Freddy lay there. Then very quietly he got up and started to tiptoe back the way he had come. In his detective work he had learned to move very quietly, and so Charles and Weedly didn't hear him, and they started to move along at about the same time. And Freddy, peering cautiously through the leaves, saw them. At least he saw Weedly's nose coming out from behind a bush and Charles's tail feathers disappearing at the same time in behind the other side of the bush. And he jumped to the conclusion that both nose and tail feathers belonged to the same animal.

It's sometimes pretty hard to tell how large things really are, if there isn't something near to them that you can measure them by. In the dim light of the woods, a squirrel can look as big as a cow, if you think he's farther away than he is. To Freddy, this queer monster with the head of a pig and a great plume of tail feathers seemed to be quite a distance away, and consequently it appeared as huge as an elephant. He gave a squeal of sheer fright and dashed off through the underbrush.

It was a good loud squeal, and it seemed louder because of the silence. Charles and Weedly looked and caught a glimpse of a whitish animal through the leaves, and then they too made a rush for the safety of the road. The three animals burst from the woods at almost the same moment, and threw themselves down panting in the grass.

"Oh, my word!" gasped Charles. "What an escape! Why, Freddy! How'd you get here?"

"You didn't meet me," said Freddy. "I went alone. Saw the Ignormus. Great white creature with a wicked long snout and a tail on him like a bird."

"We waited for you," said Weedly. "But that don't matter. We went into the Big Woods all right. Do you suppose there's two of those Ig-what-do-you-call-'ems, or did we see the same one?"

"I didn't see any tail feathers," said Charles, "but what a terrible screech he gave! Like a fire engine. Ugh!" He shuddered, and then suddenly his eyes rolled up in his head and he fell over in a dead faint.

"My goodness!" said Freddy. "Poor chap, I don't blame him. Catch hold, Weedly, and we'll carry him down to the brook where we can splash some water on him. Look out; easy with those tail feathers. If you pull any of 'em out, Henrietta'll have something to say to us, and we've had enough excitement for one day."

So they carried Charles over to the brook, and after they had splashed water on him and patted his claws and done all the things people do when anybody faints, Charles opened his eyes.

"Where am I?" he said weakly.

"You're all right, old boy," said Freddy. "Can you get up? Here, you put one wing over Weedly's shoulder and the other over mine, and we'll help you home."

It wasn't very easy for the two pigs to get the rooster down through the woods. He leaned on them heavily, and complained a good deal when they stumbled.

"Don't hurry me!" he said. "I'm doing the best I can."

"We don't want to hurry you," said Weedly, "but we think you ought to get home as soon as you can. Henrietta will be anxious about you."

"Ah, my poor Henrietta!" sighed Charles. "Little does she know what terrors her devoted husband has faced."

"You'll want to get back and tell her about it," said Freddy. "She'll be pretty proud of you, I bet. Why, you've seen the Ignormus!"

"Eh?" said Charles, perking up. "Why, that's so, isn't it? They'll all be proud of me, won't they? Oh, of you, too, of course. Maybe they'll give us a parade, eh, Freddy?" And he stopped leaning on them and darted ahead, running as fast as he could.

Freddy winked at Weedly. "We ought to have thought of that before," he said.

Chapter 6

For the next week little was talked about on the Bean farm but what came to be known as the Big Woods Exploring Expedition. Charles got the lion's share of the praise, probably because the animals had always thought of him, perhaps not exactly as a coward, but at least as a good deal better at big talk than at brave action, whereas the two pigs had both in the past shown plenty of courage. Henrietta was so pleased that she even offered several mornings to get up and crow for Charles, if he wanted to stay in bed. For hens, as you perhaps know, can crow just as well as roosters if they want to. Usually they don't want to.

But Charles wouldn't let her. "No, no, my dear," he said. "I must continue to fulfill my humble duties, just like any ordinary rooster."

The truth was that he wanted to be up and around where he could be admired. All day long he could be seen strutting about the farmyard, stopping to acknowledge graciously the praise and congratulations of his friends, or perched on a fence, delivering a short address on courage or bravery. He even went around to some of the neighboring farms and gave lectures on such topics as "Through the Big Woods with Gun and Camera," or "Tracking the Ignormus to His Lair," or "Hairbreadth Escapes of an Intrepid Explorer."

But after his fright had worn off, Freddy began to wonder what really had happened up in the Big Woods. He thought and he thought, and finally one day he made up his mind, and without saying anything to anybody he went back. The trail of crushed leaves and broken twigs where he had rushed down to the road, was easy to follow. It scared him to go into the Big Woods again, but he went on until he came to the place where he had been when he had heard the twig snap. From it, he could see the bush behind which he had seen the fearsome animal that he had taken for the Ignormus. It was nearer than he had thought. He went over to it, and then the whole thing was clear. For behind it were footmarks which could only have been made by a pig, and a small reddish feather that had probably been shaken out of Charles's wing.

"Ho hum," said Freddy. "So that was it. We scared each other." He sat down and looked at the footprints. "Just the same," he thought, "that doesn't prove that there *isn't* an Ignormus in the woods." It wasn't a very comfortable thought. He shivered and looked over his shoulder; then he tiptoed quietly back to the road.

As soon as he was out in the sunlight again

he felt better. "It's funny," he thought. "Whether I believe in the Ignormus or not depends entirely on where I am. Out here I'm perfectly sure there isn't any such creature. Am I sure?" He thought a minute. "Yes, I *am*," he said. "But the minute I step in under those trees I'll believe in him again."

He tried it to see. He went a little way into the Big Woods, but he hadn't been there more than a few minutes before he began to feel queer in the back of his neck and to peer around anxiously. "Maybe there is something here," he said. "I suppose it's sort of foolish to be here. I guess—ooh! What was that!" For something had groaned.

Freddy dashed out across the road again. And as he was lying there watching, the groan was repeated. Then he saw that it was two branches rubbing against each other in the wind. "Just the same," he said, "I think I've done enough for one day."

He had been going to tell the other animals what he had found out, but when he thought it over he saw that he couldn't. If it got out that he and Charles and Weedly had just scared each other, they'd never hear the last of it. Life just wouldn't be worth living. So he kept it to himself. But when he was asked, as he was a dozen times a day, to describe the Ignormus, he began to make his description a little less frightful. He said no, it wasn't so terrible big; maybe not much bigger than a pig. And he left off the plume of tail feathers entirely.

Finally Charles got a little angry about it. "What's the matter with you, Freddy?" he said. "Here we've had a perfectly dreadful adventure, and you talk as if it didn't amount to anything. You talk as if we'd been scared by a mouse."

"Well, maybe we were," said Freddy. "*I* didn't see anything but just something white going through the bushes. What did you see, really?"

"Well, I—well, it was a terrible great creature, champing his jaws and screaming," said Charles. "Wasn't it?" he added doubtfully.

"I don't know. Maybe that's what you saw, but I didn't see anything like that. All I mean,

Charles, is—if somebody finds out that there really *isn't* any Ignormus in the woods at all. we're going to look pretty silly."

"Pooh," said the rooster, "he's there all right."

But after that, Freddy noticed that Charles didn't describe the Ignormus much.

In the meantime, nothing more had been heard about Simon, although the army had been out patrolling the fields and the fences, and Jinx had been watching nights around the barn.

"I guess the rats know better than to come back here," said Mrs. Wiggins. "Certainly if they were living in the neighborhood, somebody would have seen them by this time."

So the next time the army came to report, she told them they weren't needed any more, and they lined up and gave three loud cheers, and then disbanded.

One evening Charles and Freddy and Jinx and his sister went down to Centerboro to the movies. Mr. Muszkiski, the manager of the movie theatre, liked to have the animals come, because it made it more interesting for the audience to have celebrities like the Bean animals in the house, and he only charged them ten cents. Since Freddy had founded the First Animal Bank, most of the animals had got together a little money which they kept in the bank vaults, and when they went to the movies they would stop in and draw out enough for their tickets, with perhaps an ice cream cone afterwards.

Tonight the picture was about pirates, and the hero dashed about fighting duels and rescuing the heroine and pitching people overboard and generally acting in a very swashbuckling and death-defying manner. Charles, who since the adventure in the Big Woods, had begun to think of himself as a good deal of a hero, got very excited. He jumped up and down on his seat. "That's it!" he shouted. "Go it! Hit him again!" And finally, in the big fight between the hero and the villain, he flew up on the back of his seat and flapped his wings and crowed.

Everybody in the audience turned around

. . . an old lady was reaching with an umbrella

and stared, and a good many of them laughed.
This made Charles mad, and paying no attention to Freddy, who was trying to get him to
quiet down, he shouted angrily: "That's right —
laugh! I guess you people don't know who I
am! Me, who's seen what I've seen and done
what I've done! Me—"

"Who's going to get slapped into a feather
duster if you don't shut up," interrupted the
cat, scooping Charles down into his seat with
one black paw. "Now, pipe down, rooster, or
I'll abolish you."

So after a protesting squawk or two, Charles
subsided.

As they were leaving the theatre, Freddy
felt a sharp poke in the back, and he turned
around. An old lady a little farther back in the
crowd was reaching forward with her umbrella
to jab him again. He recognized her at once,
and bowed politely. She was a Mrs. Lafayette
Bingle, and once when Freddy had been in the
detective business she had come to him to help
her find her spectacles, which she had mislaid.
Freddy had looked at her and said: "Why,

ma'am, they're right on your forehead." And they were, for she had pushed them up there to look at something out of the window, and forgotten them.

Mrs. Bingle had thought it very clever of Freddy to see them, and she had promised him that if she was ever able to, she would pay him well for his services. Of course Freddy hadn't wanted any pay for so small a service, but she had insisted, and so Freddy had said: "Why, all right, if you feel that way, ma'am, you can pay me some time." And then he had forgotten about it.

But now she drew him aside when they got into the street, and fumbled in her purse and brought out three ten dollar bills.

"I told you I would pay you some day for finding my spectacles," she said, "and I am happy to say that I am now able to do so, for I have just inherited two large apartment houses, three farms, and $250 from an uncle in California, and so you must take this."

"I couldn't think of it, ma'am," Freddy protested.

"You can think of it and you can do it," said Mrs. Bingle.

"A dollar would be more than enough," said Freddy. "Why, this would buy half a dozen pairs of glasses."

But Mrs. Bingle was determined, and she made such a fuss that Freddy finally accepted. "But," he said, "it is a very large fee for such a small service."

"And you," said Mrs. Bingle, "are a very important pig to ask such a small service of. Besides, I should never have found the spectacles without your help, and then I should never have been able to read the letter telling me about the two large apartment houses, and the three farms, and the $250, and so I would probably never have got them at all."

Freddy argued some more, but Mrs. Bingle was quite a character—that is, she was accustomed to having her own way. So when Freddy had thanked her, he said: "If you ever need a detective again, you shall have all the help I can give you, and I will give it free, gratis and for nothing."

Charles was pretty excited on the way home. He strutted up the middle of the road, and shouted threats and insults at passing cars when he had to jump into the ditch to keep from being run over. Once, when they were climbing a hill, a truck came up slowly behind them and Charles refused to get out of the way. He stood in the glare of the headlights, and dared the driver to come on. And the truck stopped.

"Hey, chicken, get out of the road," shouted the driver, sticking his head around the windshield. "If I hadn't thought you were a skunk, you'd be a pancake now."

"Get out of the way yourself," screamed Charles. "I've got as much right on the road as you have. Chicken, indeed! Get down and fight, if you want to get by here. I'm as good a man as you are."

"I don't doubt it," said the truck driver with a laugh. "Guess you're one of Bean's talking animals, ain't you? Hop in, you and your friends, and I'll give you a lift."

But Charles said he wouldn't ride with anyone who called him names.

"I hope you'll excuse my friend," said Freddy. "He isn't usually this way. He's been seeing too many movies."

"He won't see many more if he goes around trying to push trucks off the road," said the driver with a laugh. "Well, get him out of the way, will you?"

So Freddy and Jinx dragged the angry rooster off the road and the truck went on.

"What on earth is the matter with you, Charles?" said Freddy. "Even if you're as brave as you say you are, you can't push trucks around."

"Yeah?" said Charles. "Well, he stopped, didn't he?"

"And I suppose if he hadn't," said Jinx, "you'd have torn his tires off. This Big Woods trip of yours has gone to your head."

"It has not," said Charles. "But I don't take 'chicken' from anybody. Me, a full grown rooster! He called me a chicken. Nobody can call me that and get away with it."

"Oh, can't they!" said Jinx. He looked worriedly at his friend. "I guess we'll have to settle this right now. If you go on trying to bully people ten times your size, the Bean farm will have to find a new alarm clock in about a week. So I guess it's up to me to put you through the grinder. I say you're a chicken, Charles. Do you want to make something of it?" And he squared off and tapped Charles on the beak with his paw.

But Charles backed off. "I don't fight with my friends," he said huffily. "Anyway, I know you don't mean it."

"But I do. Chicken," said Jinx, and he tapped Charles again, harder.

"Here now, you quit," said the rooster. For a minute it looked as if he was going to back down. And then suddenly, to their surprise, he gave a squawk and spread his wings and flew at the cat.

It was pretty dark, and Freddy and Minx couldn't see very well what was going on. There was a lot of fluttering, and then Jinx said: "For Pete's sake!" and then he said: "Ouch!" And then Charles was pinned down on the road, with Jinx on top of him.

"Well, you're more of a scrapper than I thought you were, Charles," said the cat, "I'll say that for you. No, don't struggle. I'll let you up. I take back the 'chicken.' Does that satisfy you?"

Charles said it did, and Jinx helped him up and brushed him off. But Charles was still huffy, and on the way home he and Minx walked on ahead.

"Who'd have thought," said Jinx, "that a trip to the Big Woods and one little movie could turn our old wind-bag into a roaring lion? I don't like this, Freddy. He'll get into real trouble if he goes on this way."

"He's a little over himself, I'll admit," said the pig. "But he was just sounding off. Trouble was, you got him in a corner. Any animal will fight when he's cornered. We'll have to keep an eye on the old blow-hard, though. I'm kind of fond of him. I wouldn't want him to get in a mess."

As they went on down the road, they could hear Minx telling Charles about a fight she had seen in Patagonia between a parrot and a rattlesnake. "He grabbed the snake by the tail," she was saying, "and he flew up, and around, and under, and he tied the snake in a bowknot so he couldn't move. You could have done that, Charles; you're so strong and agile."

"She's putting ideas in his head," said Jinx.

"He hasn't room for more than one at a time," said Freddy. "By the way, do you mind stopping at the bank? I want to deposit this thirty dollars."

The First Animal Bank was in an old shed beside the road. As president of the bank, Freddy could go in any time of the day or night, and now he pushed open the door and woke up the squirrel who had the job of night-watchman, and who slept on the board over the hole that led down to the vaults where all the things the animals had brought in for safe-keeping were stored. The squirrel pushed aside the board, and disappeared down the hole with the envelope. But as the animals turned to go, there was a squeak of dismay, and the squirrel came scrabbling up into the shed again.

"Oh, Mr. Freddy," he panted, "the bank has been robbed!"

"Robbed!" shouted Jinx. "See here, squirrel, if all my money has been taken, there's going to be trouble. I'll hold you responsible—"

"Oh, shut up, Jinx," said Freddy. "You know you only have eighteen cents in the bank."

"No money was taken, Mr. Jinx," said the squirrel. "It's just things to eat—nuts and corn and things. The big storage room is empty, and there's a hole in the roof. They must have tunneled down from the outside."

"They?" said Freddy. "Who?"

"I don't know, sir. It's not a very big tunnel —not as big as you. It could have been woodchucks or skunks or foxes, I guess."

"When I was in Buenos Aires—" Minx began.

"Sure, sis, we know," interrupted her brother. "Bigger and better burglaries. Pipe down, will you? Let's have a look outside, Freddy."

Back of the bank was a pile of fresh dirt beside a hole which slanted down under the shed.

"That's how they did it," said Jinx. "Tough on you, Freddy. I suppose you're responsible for the safety of everything deposited in your bank, aren't you?"

"Goodness, I never thought of that," said Freddy. "I suppose I am. All next winter's supply of food for half the small animals on the farm was down there. My goodness, what'll I do?"

"I guess you'll have to catch the robbers before they eat it all up," said Jinx. "Oh, cheer up. You've done harder jobs than that in your detective work. Tell you what: it's too dark to do anything tonight. Minx and I will stay on guard here, in case they come back. And you go home and get a good night's sleep. Then in the morning we'll all get busy."

"Maybe that's best," said Freddy. "Only we must keep quiet about this until we've had a chance to look the ground over. If we get a mob of curious animals tramping over the place, there won't be a clue left. So not a word, you understand." And he looked sharply at Charles.

"You needn't look at me," said the rooster truculently. "Anybody'd think I couldn't keep a secret!"

"Anybody'd be right, too," said Jinx with a laugh; but Freddy said: "All right, Charles. I just wanted you to be careful. Now let's go home to bed."

Chapter 7

Freddy didn't sleep very well that night. The faces of all those trusting little animals who had brought their treasures into his bank for safekeeping crowded reproachfully into his dreams. For a poet to be president of the bank had always seemed to him something of a joke. For the first time he realized that it was a serious matter to be responsible for other people's property. But if he didn't catch the robbers, he'd make it good—down to the last kernel of corn.

He was at the bank early next morning, but not early enough to avoid trouble. Charles evidently hadn't been able to keep his beak shut, for word of the robbery had got out, and the building was surrounded by a mob of angry animals, who, when they saw Freddy, came streaming down the road towards him, shaking clenched paws and yelling: "We want our money!" "Give us back our belongings!"

"Please! Please!" shouted Freddy. "You'll get everything back. Let me through, will you?"

He elbowed his way to the door of the bank, and then turned and faced them. "Quiet, *please!*" he said. "You'll get everything back. Every depositor in this bank will be paid in full. But let me say first that all the money and jewelry and other things you have brought in here are safe. Only the food was taken. And I, personally, will see that you get back whatever you left here. I'll make it good if it takes my entire fortune."

"Yeah," said a voice, "and what's *that* worth?"

"I guess you may not have heard," said Freddy, "that I collected a thirty dollar fee at the movies last night. I guess that will take care of anything you've lost."

"Good old Freddy!" shouted a squirrel, and somebody proposed three cheers. But some of the animals, who, although they had not lost anything, had money or jewelry in the safe deposit vaults, were still worried.

"I thought your old bank was burglar-proof," said one of them. "If the robbers can get in once, they can get in again and steal our money."

"If you feel that your money is safer in your own homes," said Freddy with dignity, "you are at perfect liberty to take it out of the bank. We do all we can to protect the property you leave here, but there is always the possibility that a clever burglar can break in. However, I should like to point out that your own homes have no protection against burglars whatever. Here, there is always a watchman on the premises, and I may say that we plan to install a burglar alarm system this week which should give you added security."

This burglar alarm was something Freddy had thought about while he was lying awake that night. And I may say here that he did install it, and it worked very well. He hung an old dinner bell of the Beans' in the tree over the bank, and strung a cord from it down into the vaults where a mouse he had hired for the purpose was always on duty. If the mouse heard any suspicious noises, all he had to do was pull the cord and ring the bell. As you know, a dinner bell can be heard a good deal farther than any other kind of bell, even a church bell.

The animals were reassured by Freddy's promise, and after they had hung around for a while and stared at the hole made by the burglars, they drifted off home.

"Not much use looking for clues now, after this mob has been tramping all over the place," said Freddy to Jinx. "I thought we might find some footprints. Darn that rooster! We ought to have tied him up and kept him in the bank all night."

"Only way to keep him from talking," said the cat, "is to cut his head off. And I'm not sure even that would work."

"My goodness, I'm glad they all took it the way they did," said Freddy. "All their savings gone, poor things. By the way, Jinx, did you notice a stranger in the crowd—I saw him two or three times, and then when I looked for him again he was gone. A funny looking animal, with a bushy white tail and fuzzy white whiskers."

But Jinx hadn't seen anybody. "Sounds like something Minx thought up," he said.

"They say the criminal always returns to the scene of his crime," said Freddy, "and as I knew all the other animals here, I thought he might be the robber."

"Looks like a rat job to me," said Jinx, "but we haven't seen tail nor whisker of a rat anywhere around. I guess you'll have to go back in the detective business, Freddy."

Freddy didn't want to go back in the detective business much. Detectives have to do a lot of hard thinking. Of course, in writing poetry he had to do a lot of hard thinking, too, but if a poet doesn't think hard enough to make his poem come out right he can always tear it up and nobody knows about it. But if a detective doesn't think hard enough, he doesn't catch the criminal, and everybody says he's no good. Of course Freddy had always caught everybody he went after, but he never knew whether he was going to or not, and this case looked like a particularly hard one.

The first thing he did was to hire a couple of woodchucks to fill up the hole the burglars had made. Then he fixed up the burglar alarm. Then he got hold of all the rabbits who had helped him in his other cases and had them go out and see if they could find any trace of the mysterious animal with white tail and whiskers. After that he couldn't think of anything more to do, so he went home and worked on his second poem. The sentence he started with was: "Bees, bothered by bold bears, behave badly."

For nearly a week nothing happened. No trace was found of the robbers, and the mysterious white-tailed animal seemed to have vanished from the face of the earth. Freddy began to get worried. The Big Woods expedition and the robbery had caused a lot of talk, and some of the animals began to link them together and say that maybe it was the Ignormus himself who had been the burglar.

Freddy pooh-poohed the idea. "It's a well known fact," he said, "that the Ignormus (if there *is* an Ignormus) has never left the Big Woods in all the years he's been there."

"That's all right," said Mrs. Wogus, "but there's no reason why he *couldn't* leave the woods, is there? There's a lot of us that think maybe that's just what he's doing. Maybe he's got tired of staying in the Big Woods. Maybe he's hungry. I've heard some pretty queer noises around the cowbarn nights, I can tell you. Maybe he's wandering around the farm nights. We don't like to think about that, some of us. Freddy, you've got to do something."

Freddy went around and talked to some of the other animals. He found that the situation was really becoming serious. A number of the more timid animals were even talking about leaving the Bean farm and going somewhere safer to live. And Charles was going around saying that if Freddy didn't do something pretty soon, he was going to take matters into his own claws. He would call for volunteers and lead an expedition into the Big Woods and clean out the Ignormus once for all. Of course Freddy knew that this was all talk on Charles's part, but it was causing trouble all the same.

Freddy was pretty well stumped. In all the detective stories he had read, the detective always found clues, and then he chased down the clues one by one and at the end of his chase he found the criminal. But in this case there weren't any clues. It was like trying to play a game of baseball without any ball. "How can you be a detective if there isn't anything to detect?" he said bitterly to himself. "And yet I've *got* to do something." There was no use thinking any more, because he had thought all the thoughts he had, and they weren't any good.

So he decided that there was only one thing to do. The animals were already beginning to say that he couldn't be much of a detective or he'd have found the bank robbers by this time. But they'd forget all their criticism if he went up and really explored the Big Woods and proved there wasn't any Ignormus. They'd think he was wonderful.

Freddy rather liked to be thought wonderful, as who doesn't? And first he thought he'd tell everybody what he was going to do, so that if there really *was* an Ignormus and he really got eaten up, he would at least have had the fun of being praised first. But then he thought he'd better not tell them, in case he got scared and decided to turn back before he got to the Big Woods at all. And he was getting up his nerve to start when he had a really bright idea. He would wear one of the disguises he had used in his detective work. He would disguise himself as a man—a hunter. For hunters often went into the Big Woods, and the Ignormus certainly never bothered them. Probably he didn't like guns.

Mrs. Bean, who was always willing to help the animals, had cut down a couple of Mr. Bean's old suits for Freddy when he had been in the detective business. There was one of very bright yellow and green checks that had hardly been worn at all. Mr. Bean had bought it in Paris, but after he got home he didn't like it so well. He said when he wore it into Centerboro people seemed to think he was a parade or something. So Mrs. Bean made it over for Freddy and the pig really looked very nice in it. He decided to wear it now, because it seemed to him the kind of suit a well-dressed hunter would wear.

But of course if he was a hunter, he must have a gun. So before dressing he went up to the house. Jinx and Minx were lying on the kitchen porch, blinking sleepily at a grasshopper who was sitting on the rail making faces at them, and wondering if it was worthwhile to chase him. From inside came the clatter of Mrs. Bean washing up the breakfast dishes.

"Hi, cats," said Freddy. "Where's Mr. Bean?"

Jinx said he was down in the cowbarn.

"Well, look," said Freddy. "I want to get Mrs. Bean out of the house for a few minutes. Would you two put on a fight, so she'll have to come out and stop it?"

Jinx grinned. "Anything to oblige a friend," he said. "Eh, sis?" And he gave Minx a box on the ear.

"Hey, quit," said Minx. "I don't want to fight. I'm comfortable."

"Just make a lot of noise," said Freddy. "It doesn't have to be a real fight."

"You don't know Jinx," said Minx. "He's rough. —Hey, quit!" she said as Jinx cuffed her again. "Oh, you would, would you?" And in two seconds they were rolling down the steps, slapping and biting and squalling loud enough to rouse the neighborhood.

There were quick footsteps in the kitchen, and Mrs. Bean came to the door, carrying a pan of dishwater.

"Land sakes!" she said. "What's the matter with you cats? Stop it!" She followed them as they rolled down across the lawn, trying to get near enough to throw the water on them. Freddy darted into the house. Mr. Bean's shotgun was just inside the closet off the kitchen, and he grabbed it and ran out and around the corner of the house. There was a splash, and a loud squeal from both cats, as he made off towards the pigpen.

It was a pretty serious thing to borrow Mr. Bean's gun without his permission, and under ordinary circumstances Freddy wouldn't have considered it for a minute. But these circumstances were far from ordinary. And anyway, he thought, it wasn't as if he was going to shoot the gun off. Mr. Bean seldom used it and would never miss it, and he'd bring it back in a day or two and nobody'd be any the wiser. So Freddy thought.

So Freddy put on the checked suit, with a cap to match, and shouldered the gun and trudged off up towards the woods. He was a good-sized pig, but he made a very small hunter. But none of the animals he met examined him very closely. They saw the gun and promptly got behind trees and ducked

. . . and trudged off towards the woods

down holes, or if they were caught in the open, they sat still and pretended to be a stone or a bunch of grass.

At another time, Freddy would have thought this was pretty funny, but today he had serious business on his mind, and he hardly noticed the animals. He went doggedly along, his eyes on the ground, talking to himself. "The Big Woods are perfectly safe," he muttered. "I *know* they're safe. Nothing to be scared of. Nothing." And then he took a little card out of his pocket, on which, before he left home, he had typed the words: "There isn't any Ignormus." "There," he said to himself, "you see? There it is in black and white. There isn't any such animal." For Freddy, like lots of other people, believed things more easily when he saw them in print than he did when he just heard them. Even when he had printed them himself.

He went on up along the brook into the woods, reading the card every now and then to reassure himself. When he came to the pool where Theodore lived, he sat down a minute to rest. Pretty soon over the top of a lily pad across the pool he saw two large bulging eyes staring at him. He took off his cap and waved it. The eyes disappeared, there was a flash of green in the water, and the frog climbed out on the bank beside him.

"My gug-gug I mean goodness, Freddy," said Theodore, "I didn't know you in that rig. Don't you think it's a little loud?"

"Maybe," said Freddy. "Maybe. Personally, I favor a bit of color. Makes things gayer, somehow. Not that I feel especially gay myself," he added. And he told the frog where he was going.

Theodore agreed that the Ignormus certainly wouldn't bother a hunter with a gun. "I wish you'd take me," he said. "I'd feel safe with that gun to protect me."

"I'd like your company all right," said Freddy. "But whoever heard of a hunter going out with a frog?"

"I could pretend I was a dud—I mean dog,"

said Theodore. "I can bark like one." And he gave a couple of croaks, which did indeed sound rather doglike.

Freddy said that was all very well, but who ever heard of a green dog?

"Well," said the frog, "if you come to that, who ever heard of a pig in a plaid suit?"

Freddy felt that there was something wrong with Theodore's argument, but he was pretty anxious to have company. "All right," he said, "but you must promise not to be scared."

"Sure, I'll promise if you will," said the frog.

Freddy thought about that a minute, and then he said: "Well, we'll both promise to *try.*" And they set out.

Chapter 8

They went up along the brook, and Theodore dashed in and out of the bushes croaking, to seem as doglike as possible. Just before they got to the road, Freddy stopped suddenly, looking down into the water where a corncob was bobbing along on the current. "Look!" he said.

"What's so funny about that?" said Theodore.

"Good gracious," said Freddy, "don't you see what it means?"

"It means somebody threw a corncob in the water."

"Yes, but who?"

"Who!" said the frog. "How do I know? What's it matter? I've seen quite a few cobs floating down the last few days."

"It matters a lot," said Freddy. "This brook comes down from the Big Woods. Whoever threw it in the water was probably in the Big Woods. And if that isn't some of the corn that was stolen from the bank, I miss my guess."

"Oh, I see," said Theodore. "Then you think it really was the Ignormus that robbed the bank?"

"I don't believe in the Ignormus," said Freddy.

"Just because you've never seen him," said the frog. "Well, I've never seen the President of the United States, but I believe in him all right."

"I wish you wouldn't argue so much," said the pig. "And there's no use dragging the

President of the United States into this. Come on. Are we going to explore the Big Woods, or not?"

So they went on up the brook and across the road and into the gloomy silence of the Big Woods. Theodore dashed about barking in the underbrush, and several times gave Freddy quite a start by coming out unexpectedly in a different place. But in his disguise, and with a real gun over his shoulder, the pig found he wasn't as scared as he had been on his previous visits. He trudged along boldly, and really made a good deal of noise, though not any more than he could help.

There had once been a path leading to Mr. Grimby's house, but it was now so overgrown with saplings and berry bushes that it was easier not to walk on it. They went through the trees alongside it, and pretty soon began to catch glimpses of a sagging roof, and of walls from which all the paint had long since peeled off. They crept closer, and peered out from behind the bushes at the dilapidated old house.

"Hardly a whole window in the place,"

whispered Theodore. "I bet if a mouse walked over that roof he'd f-fall right through to the cellar. Just the kind of place an Ignun-nun—I mean—normus would live."

Freddy didn't like the look of the house much either. But he thought of the card in his pocket that said, "There isn't any Ignormus," and he took a firm grip on his gun, and walked out from behind the bushes. "Come on," he said firmly, and went towards the house.

There wasn't any sound. The front door was open, and through it they could see the hall, from whose walls the paper was hanging in tattered strips. Freddy started up the steps, took a look at the rotting and broken boards of the porch, and went down again.

"Afraid I'd fall through," he said, "and I've got my best suit on. You don't weigh much, Theodore. Suppose you go in and scout around."

"Not me," said the frog. "Where we go, Freddy, we g-go together."

So they walked around the house. The back door was locked, but they found that the lock of the cellar door had been torn off, and Freddy laid down his gun and lifted up the wooden flap, under which a short flight of stone steps led down into darkness. The two looked at each other.

"After you," said Theodore politely. "You're the leader of this expedition."

"Pooh," said Freddy, "I'm a hunter and you're his dog. The dog is supposed to go in and chase out the game."

"Oh, sure," said the frog. "And suppose the game chases out the d-dog?"

"Well," said Freddy, "it's just an old cellar. Probably nothing in it anyway. Dust. Old bottles. Somebody's old overalls. And more dust. I suppose there's not much sense spoiling my best suit."

"I don't see why you should spoil it," said Theodore, "unless you plan to lie down and roll on the floor."

The frog was grinning at him. "Oh, well," said Freddy, "come on, then." And holding his gun in front of him he started down the stairs.

The cellar was grim and gloomy. In it were all the things Freddy had mentioned and quite a lot more: old barrels and packing cases and broken furniture. It smelt musty, because rain from the leaky roof had dripped through on to the floor over their heads, and in one or two places the boards had broken away so they could see up into the rooms above. They were standing under one of these holes when Freddy thought he heard something move upstairs.

"Listen!" he whispered. "Sounded like something being dragged across the floor."

"Wind, probably," said Theodore. "Blowing a loose shutter."

"I think—" Freddy began. But whether he really had a thought, or was just going to say something, the frog never knew, for at that moment several things happened very rapidly.

The sound above them came again, and something long and black and wiggly dropped through the hole and came down with a slap between them. "A snake!" croaked Theodore,

That is what happened to Freddy.

and he gathered his hind legs under him and in one magnificent jump soared up through the cellar door and out into the open air. At the same moment Freddy pulled up his gun and fired.

It wasn't that Freddy was afraid of snakes. Indeed one of his best friends was a garter snake named Homer who lived down by the brook. For in his early days as a detective, Freddy had thought that if he could only glide like a snake he could follow people he was shadowing much more quietly. And so he had taken gliding lessons from Homer. He had never shown much improvement, and had finally given the lessons up, but the friendship continued, and he and Homer often took long walks together—if a snake can be said to take walks when he hasn't any legs.

But it seemed to Freddy that this snake was attacking his friend, Theodore, and so he tried to shoot him. But Freddy didn't know much about firing a shotgun. It isn't enough to just point it at the mark and pull the trigger. You have to press the butt of the gun tight into your shoulder before firing, for a shotgun kicks like a mule and if you don't hold it tight it will knock you off your feet. That is what happened to Freddy. The gun kicked back and knocked him heels over head into a pile of old boxes which came tumbling down over him, and the last box came down and hit him on the head, and that was the last he knew for quite a while.

When he came to, he didn't at first know where he was. Then he saw Theodore. The frog had waited some time before venturing back into the cellar, and I think it was very brave of him to go back at all. But frogs are pretty loyal friends. He had gone in and seen Freddy lying among the boxes, and then he had rushed out to get some water. But all he could find was an old acorn cup full of rain water. That much water doesn't go very far on a face as broad as Freddy's, and when he had sprinkled all he had on his friend, he picked up a little white feather that was lying nearby and began tickling the pig's nose. That was what brought Freddy to.

"What—what happened?" he asked.

"I don't know," said Theodore. "I wasn't here. You shot the snake, I guess."

"I remember now," said Freddy. "Then the house fell on me. I wonder if I'm badly injured." He wriggled his nose. "Thank goodness, that's all right," he said. Then he wiggled his ears. They were all right, too. Then he tried to wiggle his tail, but nothing happened. "Theodore!" he exclaimed. "My tail! It must be broken. I can't wiggle it."

"You're lying on it," said the frog.

"Oh," said Freddy. Very slowly he sat up. "My best suit!" he said sadly, looking down at it. "Hey, wait a minute," he said suddenly. "Where'd you get that feather?"

Theodore said it had just been lying there.

Now Freddy was a good detective. That is, if he saw something, he didn't just look at it as you or I would and then forget it. He thought about it and wondered what it meant. And by and by, if you think about something long enough, you begin to see things about it. Freddy saw that this feather was a very queer thing to find in a cellar, in the middle of a patch of woods where no birds had lived for years. And it wasn't an old feather, all bedraggled as it would have been if it had lain there a long time. It was fresh and fluffy. He put it in his pocket and got up.

"You got the snake anyway," said Theodore. "At least—Well, what do you know about that!" he exclaimed. For what they had thought a snake was nothing more than a short length of old rubber hose, now well riddled with birdshot.

Freddy looked down at it. "This is getting beyond me," he said. "A snake, I could understand. But a piece of hose doesn't jump through a hole in the ceiling all by itself. And what's this on it?" He bent and picked up a small piece of paper. "Warning!" he read. "In this house pigs become pork. This means you! (Signed) The Ignormus."

"Hey, let's get out of here," said Theodore.

"Yes," muttered the pig. "Guess you're right. Just as soon as I get my—Why, where's the gun?"

The gun had vanished.

"Maybe under the boxes," said Freddy, and began pulling them about. "You go on if you want to, Theodore, but I'd rather face sixteen Ignormuses with pink eyes than Mr. Bean if he knows I borrowed his gun."

But the gun wasn't under the boxes. And though Freddy hunted thoroughly, it wasn't in the cellar.

"Maybe it flew out of the door," said Theodore. "Look, it's getting late. It will be dark before we get out of the Big Woods if we don't hurry. I'm going."

There was nothing else for Freddy to do. An angry Mr. Bean might be worse than the Ignormus, but the Big Woods at night seemed right now worse than either of them. But he'd have to come back tomorrow and find the gun.

By the time they got to the road it was indeed beginning to get dark. They sat down a minute and rested, because they had run pretty fast.

"You know, Theodore," said Freddy, "you haven't stammered once since we got to that house. Do you suppose it got scared out of you?"

The frog grinned. "I guess I forgot it," he said. "I don't really have to stammer, Freddy. I did a little, when I was a tadpole, but I got over it. Only I found that it was pretty useful. You see, when anybody asks you a question, sometimes you can't think of an answer right away. But if you begin sort of stammering and stuttering around, it gives you time to think up a really good one."

"My goodness," said Freddy, "that's a smart; idea. Only if everybody stammered until they thought up just what they wanted to say, there wouldn't be much conversation."

"No," said Theodore, "but what there is would be better. That's why I like to live up here in the woods. I don't hear so much talk."

"You'd like Mr. Bean, then," said Freddy. "He hardly ever says anything. Oh, dear, why did I think of Mr. Bean? What he'll say when he finds his gun is missing I hate to think."

"You just said that he hardly ever says anything," put in Theodore.

"I guess that's what I'm afraid of. He won't talk; he probably won't even give me a licking."

"Well, then, I don't see what you're so scared of."

"It's what he'll think," said Freddy. "Whenever I see him around the barnyard, he'll look at me reproachfully, and I'll know he's thinking: 'I'm disappointed in Freddy. I thought he was an honest pig.' You know, Theodore, that'll hurt more than all the lickings in the world."

"No, I don't know," said the frog. "I got licked plenty when I was a tadpole, and it hurt all right. There was a lily pad down at the foot of the pool, and when we'd been bad my father used to haul us out on it and take us across his knee and spank us. There were about fifty of us, so it kept him pretty busy, and finally he gave it up. He said he was doing so much spanking that he was neglecting his business, and we'd just have to get along without it. We were all a lot happier after that, and it's a funny thing, but we behaved better too."

But Freddy wasn't listening. He had taken his coat off and was brushing the dust off it with a wisp of grass. Now he put it on. "Well," he said, "I guess I'd better go down and face the music. See you tomorrow, Theodore."

He went down along the brook. Now that he had no gun the animals didn't hide from him, and those that he passed looked at him curiously, but none of them recognized him. It occurred to him that it would be fun to see if any of his friends recognized him. So when he saw a small group of animals by the corner of the cowbarn he went towards them.

Minx was apparently bragging about something to Mrs. Wiggins and to the two dogs, Robert and Georgie. Freddy heard her say: "Oh yes, when I lived there I had a whole pint of cream every day in a silver bowl. It was a wonderful big house—much bigger than the Bean house—more like a palace, really—" She stopped as Freddy came up.

He touched his hat politely. "Pardon me," he said, "but would ye be so kind as to tell an ould man if 'tis the good Beans that do be livin' in yonder house?" He spoke in a strong Irish brogue to disguise his voice.

The animals as a rule did not like to have strangers know they could talk, so they didn't say anything.

"Deary me," said Freddy, "'tis many a long road I have traveled to reach this place and see with me own eyes the talkin' animals. A wonder of the world they are, I've heard tell. But if 'tis all a story made up by them that writes for the newspapers, and no truth in it, why 'tis a bitter disappointment, so it is." And Freddy took out a rather grimy pocket handkerchief and held it to his eyes.

This was too much for Mrs. Wiggins, who was one of the softest hearted cows that ever lived. "Land sakes," she said; "we can talk. Here, stop it! or you'll have me crying too, and believe me, when I cry, I *cry*!"

Freddy knew this was true. When Mrs. Wiggins cried you could hear her down in Centerboro, and it was almost impossible to make her stop. So he took the handkerchief down. "Oh, ma'am," he said delightedly, "'tis true, then! You do talk! And would ye say a few words that I can be after takin' back to Ireland with me to tell my grandchildren how I heard the wonderful talking animals?"

"I lived in Ireland once, mister," said Minx.

"O'Houlihan's the name," said Freddy. "And did ye now? A talking cat, no less! Ah, it's the fine pretty kitty ye are too!" And he patted Minx kindly on the head.

"I lived in Dublin," said the cat. "In a great big beautiful house on Gratton Street. It had seventy windows, and in every window was a silk cushion I could sit on."

"And may I make so bold as to ask whose house that was?" said Freddy.

"It belonged to Mr. Shaemus O'Toole."

"I know that house fine!" exclaimed Freddy. "'Twas the little gatehouse to me own fine big estate. I gave it to me grandchildren for a playhouse."

"I guess you're thinking of the wrong house," said Minx. "This house had seventy windows; it was big—"

"Sure, 'twould seem big to a cat," said

Freddy kindly. "Seventy windows it had, and the cushions and all. But me own house had three hundred and forty-two windows not countin' the top floor, and in each of them a great soft divan upholstered in red plush with green fringe. A nice little place, if I do say it meself."

"Oh," said Minx, and the other animals looked at her and grinned. Then she said: "Well, I didn't mean that that was the nicest house I've ever lived in."

"Oh, sure, sure," said Freddy. "A little dump like that! A fine cat like you must have lived in some real nice places. Palaces, no less."

"I was just telling the others," said Minx, "about a prince's palace I lived in Rome. Where I had a pint of real cream every day in a silver bowl."

"Did you now?" said Freddy. "Sure, them princes are stingy people. I mind when I was in Rome. The Parchesi Palace I lived in— 'tis the biggest palace in all Italy. Me little nephew had two kittens, and we bought a dairy farm to keep 'em supplied with cream, and then an ice cream factory to make it up in different flavors for 'em. Every morning 'twas delivered fresh—twenty-five great shiny gold cans, in the courtyard, two of cream, and twenty-three of assorted flavors of ice cream. And a man in a general's uniform to ladle it out for 'em."

"There—there must have been a lot left over," said Minx.

"There was," said Freddy. "There was. But when there was too much, we'd give a party. Just for cats. I've seen eight hundred cats sittin' in the great palace banqueting hall, bein' served ice cream by footmen in blue plush breeches and powdered wigs. 'Twas quite a sight."

"I—I guess it was," said Minx feebly.

"Sure, tell us about some more of the fine places you've lived in, me handsome kitty-cat," said Freddy.

"No-no," said Minx. "I guess I won't now."

"In that case," said Freddy, taking off his cap, and laying aside his Irish brogue, which wasn't very good anyway, "I'll just thank you for the entertainment and go on home."

"Freddy!" said Mrs. Wiggins. "Well, who'd have thought it!"

"Pooh!" said Minx. "I knew him all the time! "

"Yes, you did!" said Georgie.

"I did so!" sputtered the cat. "I guess I can tell a pig from a man! Why, once when I lived in Paris, there was a pig dressed up as a—"

"Sure, was there indeed?" interrupted Freddy, putting on his cap again and bending down close to Minx. "I remimber him well. Me own brother, he was. And was his uniform blue with white stripes?"

"Oh, keep still," said Minx crossly. "If you're just going to make fun of me, I won't tell you any more."

"Fine," said Freddy, taking off his cap again. "That's just what we wanted. Well, goodnight, all." And he strolled off.

Chapter 9

When he had taken off his disguise and folded it carefully away in moth balls, Freddy went up to the house. "Might as well get it over," he thought. But Mr. Bean was sitting on the kitchen steps, peacefully smoking his after-supper pipe. Evidently he hadn't discovered the loss of the gun. So the pig went down to the cowbarn to talk over his discoveries with Mrs. Wiggins, who had been his partner in the detective business. Mrs. Wiggins wasn't brilliant—few cows are—but she had common sense, which Freddy had found by experience was a good deal more helpful.

"Looks as if the Ignormus was in the house when you were in the cellar," she said. "And he tried to scare you with the hose, and with that warning note. And yet—"

"Yes?" said Freddy.

"Well," said the cow, "it doesn't make sense. By all accounts, the Ignormus is pretty terrible to look at. Something like a hippopotamus with wings and horns, I gather. Now why should an animal like that take the trouble to push pieces of hose around and write notes? Why wouldn't he just come to the head of the cellar stairs and say, 'Grr-r-r!'"

"Golly!" said Freddy. "That's right. You mean—?"

"Gracious, I don't know what I mean." said the cow. "I just say what I think. You're smart. It's up to you to find out what I mean. It just seems to me that if I were as ferocious looking as all that I'd be proud of it. I wouldn't hide in the woods and just let people wonder what I looked like. I'd come out and show myself and scare 'em into fits."

"Maybe he's ashamed of being so homely," said Freddy.

"Who's to say he's homely, when there's only one of him? If he had brothers and sisters, why some might be homelier than others. Take cows, now. I know that, as a cow, I'm not specially handsome. No real style, you might say."

"I think you have lots of style," said Freddy politely.

"Then you're not as smart as I think you are," said Mrs. Wiggins. "What I mean is, if I were the only cow in the world, I might go around thinking I was pretty good looking, because there wouldn't be any other cows to compare me to. And the Ignormus may be the same way. He doesn't know what a good looking Ignormus really looks like."

"I see what you mean," said the pig. "Well then, if he's not ashamed of being homely, why did he go to all the trouble of writing that note, when he could have scared us worse by just letting us see him?"

"My guess is," said Mrs. Wiggins, "that he isn't ferocious looking at all."

"Well," said Freddy, "I've never believed that there was an Ignormus. Not really. But the next thing to there not being one, is being one who is little and timid. My goodness," he said suddenly, "remember that funny animal with white tail and whiskers I told you was down at the bank? Could that be him?"

"Why not? And maybe that white feather you found was out of his tail."

"Animals don't have feathers," said Freddy.

"You mean you've never seen one with feathers," said the cow. "But you've never seen the Ignormus either, so how can you tell?"

"I guess I'd better go back and think this over," said Freddy. He went down to the pig-pen, and settled himself comfortably in his old rocking chair with his hind trotters on the desk beside the typewriter, and sank into deep thought.

When he woke up the level rays of the rising sun were trying to get through the dusty window panes beside his chair, and turning them to gold. "My goodness," he said to himself, "I've been thinking all night!" He sat up and rubbed his eyes, and then suddenly jumped up and ran to the door, for someone had knocked. "Hello, Robert," he said. "Well, this is an early call. What's on your mind?"

The big collie came in and sat down. "Plenty," he said. "I suppose you haven't heard, since you just woke up."

"Oh, I wasn't asleep," said Freddy. "Been sitting here thinking out a problem all night."

"Well, then maybe *you* heard something during the night. Footsteps—somebody moving around?"

"Can't say I did. But you see, when I'm thinking, I'm pretty concentrated. Outside noises just don't mean anything to me."

"I guess I was thinking the same way last night," said the collie. "Anyway, a lot of oats were stolen from Hank's bin, and two of Mrs. Bean's best sheets and Mr. Bean's two Sunday shirts off the line, and Mr. Bean's gun from the closet off the kitchen. How they ever got the gun I don't know, for Georgie and the two cats and I were all asleep in the kitchen. We might not have heard anybody in the barn, or out in the yard, but I don't see how a thief could come through the kitchen and not wake us. But he did."

"Mr. Bean's gun, eh?" said Freddy. His legs felt weak, and he sat down quickly in the rocker.

"Yes. And Mr. Bean's pretty mad about it. He just looked at Georgie and me and said: 'Thought you two were watch dogs!' And then he puffed on his pipe until I thought he'd set his whiskers afire, and went out to the barn. It's terrible, Freddy. I've had the job as watchman on this place for eight years, but nothing like this has ever happened before."

Freddy gave a deep sigh. "Well," he said, "I can explain about the gun. I took it."

"*You* took it!" Robert exclaimed.

So the pig explained. "It isn't right," he

said when he had finished, "for you and Georgie to be blamed for it. I'll go see Mr. Bean and tell him now."

"Wait a minute," said Robert. "Even if you tell him about the gun, there's the oats and the washing for him to be mad about. If you could get busy and detect where they were, and bring them back, and maybe the gun too, why he wouldn't get mad at you, and he wouldn't be mad at us any more."

So Freddy decided maybe that was best. He was perfectly willing to own up about the gun, but he would have to talk to Mr. Bean if he did, and Mr. Bean was rather old-fashioned and didn't think that animals should talk. It always made him uneasy when one of them forgot this and said "Good morning" to him. He thought animals should be seen and not heard.

So Robert and Freddy went up to the barn. A lot of the animals were standing around discussing the robbery. They made way for Freddy, eyeing him respectfully, and he heard someone say: "Oh, I'm glad *he's* come! He's the great detective, you know. He'll soon find out who the thief is."

Hank, the old white horse, was standing beside the oat bin. "Well, Freddy," he said, "this is a fine how-de-do."

"Pretty serious," said the pig. "Now, Hank, did you see or hear anything during the night that made you suspect anything was going on?"

"Can't say as I did," replied the horse. "You can't hardly expect me to see much in a dark barn at night, specially as I was asleep and had my eyes shut."

"Were there any suspicious noises?" asked Freddy.

"Plenty of 'em. But you know how it is; all noises at night are suspicious. And this old place is full of 'em—creakings and crackings and scamperings and groanings. Laws, if I paid any attention to 'em, I wouldn't get a wink of sleep."

"Not much help to be got out of you," said Freddy. "Well, here's some oats spilled on the floor. And some more over there. That shows the way the thief went. Let's look outside."

"Aha!" he said importantly when he had pushed through the crowd of animals by the door. "Here's another lot. Well, if the thief was as careless as that all the way home, we can find out who he was, all right."

The trail was very easy to follow. Every little ways a few grains of oats had been dropped, and Freddy walked along steadily across the barnyard, followed by the crowd of admiring animals.

"Isn't he just wonderful?" said Alice. "I saw those oats myself, but I never thought what they meant."

"Freddy reminds me at times so much of our Uncle Wesley," said Emma. "He's so quick at seeing things. Of course he hasn't the dignity, the—the distinguished air."

"Well," said her sister, "you could hardly expect that from a pig."

The route taken by the thief, however, first began to puzzle Freddy, and then to alarm him. For it went straight down to the pigpen.

There were two rooms to the pigpen: the large room that Freddy called his study, and a smaller room at the back called the library, in which he stored extra disguises, old account books from the bank, and his Complete Works of Shakespeare in One Volume. There was a little door from the outside into the library, and right in front of it was a handful of oats. And it was here that Freddy made his mistake.

Instead of opening the door, he stopped and turned to the other animals. "Guess this is a blind trail," he said. "Whoever stole the oats must have made it to mislead us, and then carried off the oats in some other direction. We'd better go back and try again."

"Well, I dunno," said Hank. "If a trail leads up to a door, and the door's shut, the natural thing is to open it, isn't it? I dunno, but it seems that way to me."

"Pshaw! " said Freddy. "The robbers would hardly hide things they stole right in the detective's own house, would they?"

"Doesn't seem so," said Robert. "Not if the

"You may well say 'For goodness sakes!'"

detective was sitting up all night, thinking. So why *not* open the door?"

"Sheer waste of time," grumbled Freddy. "But if you insist—" And he flung the door open. On the floor was a bundle of something tied up in a sheet. Jinx ran forward and clawed one corner loose, and a trickle of oats ran out.

"Well, for goodness sake!" said Freddy weakly.

"You may well say 'For goodness sake!'" remarked Henrietta drily. "I guess you may do a little explaining, too, Freddy."

"Explaining!" said Freddy. "What can *I* explain? This is as much of a surprise to me as it is to you. I wish somebody *would* explain it."

"Doesn't look to me so hard to explain," said Robert, looking severely at the pig. "Looks to me as if you were a little careless, letting those oats spill out when you were carrying them down here last night."

"Me?" exclaimed Freddy. "You think that *I* stole them? What on earth would I do with oats? Pigs don't eat oats."

"No," said the dog, "but you've got to pay

back oats and corn and nuts and things to all the animals that lost their property in the bank robbery. You could use the oats for that. Then you wouldn't have to spend the money you earned."

"Rubbish!" said Freddy crossly. "The robbers just planted this stuff in my house to make it look as if I'd stolen it. Are you animals going to be foolish enough to fall for a trick like that?"

He looked around at his friends, but they all shook their heads doubtfully. "It looks funny, Freddy," said Hank, and Robert said: "You told me you were awake all night. Wouldn't you have heard the robbers, then, if they were dragging this sheet in here, just on the other side of a thin partition?"

"Well, I don't know that I was awake all night," said Freddy. "I no doubt dropped off for a few minutes now and then. When I'm thinking out some difficult problem, I find that it helps to knock off thinking and take a little nap. And then go at it fresh again."

He tried to make it sound as reasonable as

possible, but Henrietta said: "Pooh! Why didn't you open this door right away, then, if you were so innocent?"

"To tell you the truth, I was afraid of finding just what we did find. When the trail of oats led to my door, I knew pretty well what to expect, and I knew you'd be suspicious of me."

"Well, we are all right," said Henrietta bluntly.

"You admit yourself you took the gun," said Robert. "Why wouldn't we think you took the other things, too? We know you, Freddy, and we're all fond of you, but you must admit things look very queer."

"Well—" said Freddy, and then he stopped. For there came Mr. Bean, following the trail of oats from the barn. He came along slowly— though not as slowly as Freddy had—and he came to the open door, and he looked in, and he saw the oats. He puffed hard at his pipe for a minute, and then he looked at all the animals in turn, and last he looked at Freddy. "Humph!" he said disgustedly. "Stealing, hey? I wouldn't have thought it of you . . ." Then he shook his head sadly and turned back to the house. And after looking sympathetically at Freddy for a minute, the animals followed him.

Up to this point Freddy's friends hadn't really been very serious in all the things they had said. They had felt that it was rather fun to catch the pig in an embarrassing position, but they hadn't really believed that he had stolen the oats. But when Mr. Bean seemed so sure, some of them began to be doubtful. "No robber is going to take the trouble to steal oats and then hide them in the pigpen, instead of taking them home and eating them," they said. "And why should anyone want to cast suspicion on Freddy anyway? What would it get them?"

"Oh, pooh," said Jinx. "Who ever heard of a detective detecting himself. If he'd stolen the things, he wouldn't lead everyone right to where he'd hidden them." But still the animals were doubtful. So Jinx turned back.

"Look, Freddy," he said, "we're for you.

We know you're no thief. But just the same there will be a lot of talk, and you're going to be the unpopular pig around here unless you catch the thief."

"You're telling me," said Freddy, bitterly. He seldom used slang, and it shows how upset he was that he used it now.

"Yes, I am," said the cat. "You've got to get busy. Come on, Freddy. You know what they used to say about you: Freddy always gets his animal. Trot out the old Sherlock Holmes stuff. I'm with you to the last claw. I'm not much at detecting, but if it comes to a scrap—boy, Jinx is there!" And he arched his back and spat ferociously.

Freddy laughed. "I haven't exactly been idle," he said, "though I don't know that what I've found out makes much sense. But come into the study and let me tell you about my last trip to the Big Woods."

So they went into the study and Freddy hung a sign on the outside of the door which said: In Conference: Do Not Disturb. Farm animals are very curious, and if when they saw this sign they had really thought there was a conference going on, they would have come in with some excuse or other in order to get in on it. But they had learned by experience that when the sign was there, Freddy was usually asleep. And that, of course, was nothing to be curious about. So Freddy was pretty sure they wouldn't be interrupted.

Chapter 10

A couple of hours before this conference started, Mr. Webb, the spider, had set out from the cowbarn where he lived with Mrs. Webb, to call on Freddy. Usually when he had something to tell Freddy, he would swing down a long strand of his web onto the nose of one of the cows, and if she didn't sneeze and blow him halfway across the barn, he would walk up to her ear and ask her to get Freddy to come see him. But this was a confidential matter, and after talking it over with Mrs. Webb, he decided that the best plan was to see Freddy himself.

From the cowbarn to the pigpen wouldn't have been a long walk for you or me, but for a spider it was a tiring and even rather perilous journey. Getting through the grass of the barnyard was like forcing a way through a jungle. He had to push and clamber with all eight legs working hard. When a grass stalk leaned in the direction he was going, he could climb it and walk to the end and drop off, maybe six inches or a foot farther on. And there was always the danger that some careless animal might step on him.

But Mr. Webb was a courageous insect, and where duty was concerned nothing was allowed to stand in his way. He climbed up on to the outside of Freddy's study window just three hours after setting out. "And very good time too," he panted, and then without waiting to catch his breath he began walking up and down the window to attract the pig's attention.

The window was so dirty that Mr. Webb couldn't see in, but he knew by the sound of voices that Freddy was there. Then he realized that if he couldn't see Freddy, Freddy couldn't see him, so he slipped through a crack above the window and walked up on to the ceiling of the study. Then he spun a long strand and dropped down on it, and began swinging back and forth between the two animals, who were deep in conversation.

At first they didn't notice him, then Jinx saw something swoop past his nose and, thinking it was a fly, made a pass at it. Luckily he missed, and as the spider swung back, Freddy said: "Why, it's Webb! Hello, Webb; you're surely not hunting for flies in this beautifully spick and span apartment, are you?"

Mr. Webb swung himself down on to Freddy's nose, and then walked up almost into his ear. Spiders have very small voices, and they have to be almost in your ear before you can hear them, which is probably why so few people have ever heard a spider say anything.

"Listen, Freddy," he said, "if this place is

spick and span, I'm a tarantula. If you'd wash
your windows once a year, I wouldn't have to
risk my life trying to attract your attention."

"I'm dreadfully sorry," said the pig, "but
you know how it is, Webb. Time goes by, and
there are so many little household duties—"

"Never mind that," interrupted the spider.
"Can you come up to the cowbarn right away?
There's a beetle up there who's got some in-
formation I think you should have. I came
down to tell you myself because it's about the
Ignormus."

"The Ignormus!" Freddy exclaimed.
"Who is this beetle? Where is he?"

"I guess you don't know him. His name's
Rudolph or Ransom or something. He lives
up by the brook. He's down in the bug swing
now."

"The bug swing?" said Freddy. "Never
heard of it."

"Well," said the spider, "when Mr. Bean
gave you animals that swing, the bugs thought
they'd like to have one too, so me and mother,
we spun 'em one. Two thick strands down

from the cowbarn rafters, and fastened 'em to a chip for the bugs to sit in. But you'll see it when you get there."

Jinx hadn't of course heard anything Mr. Webb said, and he was jumping up and down with curiosity. Cats always pretend they aren't interested in what is going on, and they turn away and wave their tails to show how indifferent they are. But some time you try doing something where your cat can't quite see what you're up to, and you'll find out quickly how curious he is.

So when Freddy had told Jinx, they went up to the cowbarn. The bug swing was very popular. Before they got in the door they could hear the chirping and trilling of excited insects, and a long line of bugs of all kinds, waiting for their turn, extended halfway across the barnyard. The swing was hung pretty high, and from its seat a long strand of web ran up to a rafter on which Mrs. Webb was sitting. She would pull the seat up to the rafter, a bug would get on, and then she would let go and the bug would swoop down and up, down and up, until Mrs. Webb thought he had had enough. Then she would pull the swing up again, and another bug would climb on. Of course some of the bugs lost their hold and fell off, but bugs are pretty light and none of them got hurt. Mrs. Wogus, who was just under the swing, didn't like it much when they fell on her, as they frequently did.

"It's been practically raining bugs in here, Freddy, for the last two days," she said. "Can't you get 'em to move that thing somewhere else? I've got nothing against bugs, but I must say it isn't very pleasant to have a continual procession of them walking down your backbone."

"Mother and I are going to fix that," said Mr. Webb, who was still sitting in the pig's ear. "We're going to weave a net across tomorrow, and when they fall, they'll fall into that."

So Freddy explained to the cow, while Mr. Webb jumped down and went over to the waiting line. He came back in a minute, followed by a large and rather clumsy beetle. who stumbled a good deal and even fell down twice before he reached Freddy, who put his head down close to the floor and said: "I guess Mr. Webb needn't bother to introduce us. He said you had something to tell me."

"Pleased to meet you," said the beetle in a hoarse but perfectly audible voice. "My name's Randolph. You must excuse me falling down so much, but you see it's kind of a family failing. All the family—got too much of everything. Too many legs, too many wings. Look at me, now. Got four wings, but can I fly? No, sir. Come down like a kite with its tail off as soon as I try. And the same with walking. Got six legs, and what can I do with 'em? If I had four, same as you, sir, I could manage. As it is, there's always four that's walking and two that's tripping the others up."

"I'm sorry to hear it," said Freddy as the beetle paused for breath. "It must be very trying. But just what was it you had to tell me?"

"Give me time, can't you?" said the beetle testily. "I'm coming to it. Don't push me.

"Sorry," said Freddy. "But you understand, of course, that there have been some robberies on the farm, and I'm pretty anxious to clear them up as soon as possible."

"Worse than robberies," said Randolph. "There's intimidation and threats. That's what I have to tell you. But to get back to my legs. They keep throwing me. And sometimes I land on my back. When I do that, I'm stuck. Too flat to roll over, and too round to reach out and push myself. Have to wait till someone comes along and gives me a lift. Darn nuisance, but that's the way I'm built. Well, yesterday I was taking a little stroll up along the brook—if you can call it a stroll when you fall down every two feet. You know the Widow Winnick?" he asked suddenly.

Freddy knew the Widow Winnick very well. She was an elderly rabbit who lived with her dozen or so of growing children in a rather inconvenient rabbit hole up on the edge of the woods. Finding her son, Egbert, had been the first detective case the pig had ever had. "Why, yes," he said. "But what's she got to do with your legs?"

"Coming to that, coming to that," said Randolph testily. "Don't push me. Well, then, you know the widow's front door is under a big rock. Fine view from the top of that rock. Finest view in the county. Some people have no eye for landscape. Take my friend Jeffrey. He's a thousand legger. Wonderful how he can travel along with all those legs when I get all mixed up with only six. But along he goes, like a little train of cars, never stumbling, never out of step with himself. Wonderful control."

Freddy had been pretty impatient, but like all poets he was easily turned aside from any purpose by the appearance of something new, and the problem of Randolph's legs interested him. "The secret is," he said, "not to watch your legs when they're walking along. I bet you watch yours all the time."

"Think I'm a fool?" demanded the beetle. "Course I do. How do I know where the clumsy things would take me if I didn't keep an eye on 'em?"

"Well," said the pig, "the trouble is that you can't watch six legs all at one time. I think that's why you get mixed up. Go on, try it. This floor is pretty smooth. Shut your eyes and start off. I'll see you don't run into anything."

"How can I shut my eyes when I haven't got any eyelids?" said Randolph.

"Then look at the ceiling," said Freddy.

So Randolph looked up at the ceiling. "Go on, legs," he growled. "Do your stuff or I'll chew you off." And to his great surprise, as well as to Freddy's, he went swiftly across the floor without stumbling once.

"Well, upon my soul!" he said. "You've hit it, pig. Must be getting along now. Must tell Jeffrey about this." And he started out the door.

"Hey, wait a minute," said Freddy. "You were telling me something."

"To be sure," said the beetle, turning back. "H'm, where was I? Oh, yes; Jeffrey."

"On the rock," said Freddy.

"Ho, no use taking Jeffrey up on the rock. He's no more feeling for landscape than an angleworm. No soul, I tell him."

"I mean you were up on the rock yesterday," said Freddy patiently.

"So I was. Climbed up to refresh my soul
with the broad sweep of the Bean acres. Well,
I didn't refresh it much. Slipped when I got to
the top and tumbled straight down the hole
into the widow's front parlor. On my back,
too. I shouted and yelled for help but nobody
heard me, and then I heard voices out in the
kitchen. Didn't want to listen. 'Tisn't man-
ners, when folks don't know you're around.
But what could I do?

"'My, my, this is terrible,' says the widow,
and I heard her sniffling. Nothing unusual
about that; rabbits cry a lot anyway. That's
what makes their eyes red. 'Read it to me
again, Egbert,' she says.

"So I heard a piece of paper crackling and
then this Egbert began to read. It ran something like this: 'Leave one dozen prime carrots under the bridge where the brook comes
out from the Big Woods Thursday afternoon.
If you do this, and say nothing about it to anybody, nothing will happen to you. If you do

not do it, or if you mention this letter to anybody, I, the Ignormus, will come eat you up.
(Signed) The Ignormus.'

"Well," continued Randolph, "when I
heard that I thought I'd better listen some
more. 'Dear, dear,' says the widow, 'wherever
will we get a dozen prime carrots, when we
haven't so much as an old head of lettuce in
the house for supper?' 'I'll just have to steal
'em from Mr. Bean's garden,' says Egbert.
'Oh, that would be awful!' says the widow.
'What would your sainted father say if he
knew that his little Egbert, his favorite child,
was a thief?' 'I guess he'd rather have him a
thief than an Ignormus's supper,' says Egbert.
'You leave it to me, ma.'

"Well, that was all I heard, because just
then some of the other children came home,
and they saw me and turned me right side up.
So I came up here and got Webb to send for
you."

"And I'm very glad you did," said Freddy.
"This ought to give us something to go on."

"Call on me for any help you want," said

Randolph. "Glad to be of service. Don't like robbers."

"You might be some help at that," said Freddy, who was too good a detective to turn down any offers of assistance, however small. "Let me see, have I your address?"

"Third stone above the apple tree, left side of the brook going up. Just knock twice and I'll come out. If I'm not there, leave a message. My old mother's always home."

So Freddy thanked him again, and he scuttled off.

Then Freddy and Jinx went up to call on Mrs. Winnick. She was sitting in front of her doorway, wiping her eyes.

It always made Jinx mad to see anybody cry. He never cried himself, for he said it was a great waste of time. "If I feel bad about something," he said, "I go claw somebody. Then I feel better." So when he saw Mrs. Winnick he gave a disgusted sniff. "Come, come," he said; "your troubles will only grow if you water 'em. Turn off the sprinkler, will you?"

"Don't mind him, ma'am," said Freddy.

"Are you in trouble? Perhaps we can help."

"Oh, dear!" said Mrs. Winnick. "Oh, dear!"

"If you're just crying because you enjoy it," said Jinx, "tell us, and we won't spoil the fun."

"I'm in trouble," said the widow. "Great trouble. But I can't tell you what it is. I just have to bear it alone." And she sobbed openly.

Jinx started to say something, but Freddy gave him a surreptitious kick, and said: "Well, now, I don't believe it's as bad as that. Let's see if we can't guess what it is. Did you get a threatening letter maybe?"

Mrs. Winnick gulped and looked up quickly. "Why how—how did you know?" she asked, and then quickly: "Oh, no; n-nothing like that."

"Possibly," said Freddy gently, "from the Ignormus?"

"Oh, dear!" said Mrs. Winnick again, and then she burst into a flood of tears. "Oh, I did," she sobbed. "And we don't know what to do. But how could you know about it?"

"Oh, I have my ways, ma'am, of finding out

things," said Freddy airily. For like all good detectives, he never let on that what he knew was just something somebody had told him. He pretended that he had found it out in some very mysterious way. "Hadn't you better show me the letter?" he said.

So Mrs. Winnick dove down the hole and came back with the letter.

"H'm, ha!" said Freddy importantly. "Very significant."

"What's significant?" said the cat. "It's just a letter."

"Ah, my friend," said the pig, "that's just where you're wrong. To the eye of the trained detective, *nothing* is ever *just* what it seems to be."

"What does that make you?" said the cat.

But without paying any attention to the remark, Freddy went on. "The writing on this letter, you observe," he said, "is just like that on the other note—the one I got in the Big Woods. We can assume, therefore, that it was written by the same person."

"Wonderful," said Jinx sarcastically.

. . . and fell over in a faint

"Now the question is," pursued the pig, "is that person the Ignormus? But can the Ignormus (if there is an Ignormus) write? Where could he have learned to write? He has always lived in the Big Woods, we are told. Did he go to school? But if he is as terrible as they say he is, he'd have scared the children, and we'd have heard of it. On the other hand—"

"Look, Freddy," interrupted Jinx, "here's the note. Well, he can write, then. So what? You're not getting anywhere."

Freddy, who had been talking that way mainly to impress Mrs. Winnick, looked a little embarrassed, and then said: "Well, maybe you're right. Just the same, there is one thing about this letter that's funny. I've seen that handwriting before somewhere."

But Jinx wasn't impressed. "Sure," he said. "Probably you taught the Ignormus to write. You've taught a lot of animals on this farm. Probably he isn't a big animal with horns and claws, or a little animal with white whiskers. Probably he's just someone we see around all the time. You know, Freddy, I've always had a hunch that *you* were the Ignormus."

At this Mrs. Winnick gave a weak squeak and fell over in a faint.

"Now see what you've done trying to be so funny," said the pig, as he bent over the rabbit and fanned her with the letter. "That kind of smart remark is dangerous. People might get to repeating it.— There, ma'am, there," he said, as the widow opened her eyes and looked dazedly up at him. "Jinx didn't mean it. Now you go back into the house and leave everything to me."

They had some trouble persuading Mrs. Winnick to go in the house. She seemed to want to stay outdoors and cry some more. But by promising to deliver the carrots as the Ignormus had requested, they finally quieted her fears.

"Now," said Freddy, "we must get those carrots. Today is Thursday. We mustn't let the Ignormus (if there is an Ignormus) eat up Mrs. Winnick and her fourteen children."

"I expect he'd like carrots better anyway," said Jinx. "I know I would."

Chapter 11

As they came down along the stone wall towards the vegetable garden, the two animals suddenly stopped and crouched down. For among the cabbages two white ears were sticking up, where no ears ought to be. And there was a decided ripple among the beet tops, although there was no wind. Also, the small dark figure of some animal was being very busy among the onions.

"My goodness," whispered Freddy, "if Mr.

Bean saw this he'd be wild! What's got into all these animals anyway? They know perfectly well they're never allowed in the vegetable garden."

"Let me sneak in and grab one," said Jinx. "We'll soon find out."

So he got down close to the ground and crept silently in between the bean rows and disappeared. There was a squeak and a flurry among the onions, and after a minute Jinx came out, carrying a very small and very terrified squirrel by the nape of the neck. He set him down in front of Freddy.

"Well, young man," said the pig severely, "can you give me some explanation of your strange and reprehensible actions?"

"Yes, sir," stammered the squirrel. "I mean, no, sir. My actions are not rep—what you said. I was just—sort of—looking around."

Freddy bent down and sniffed. "As I thought," he said. "You've been eating onions. Mr. Bean's onions," he added more sternly. "Mr. Bean's *best* onions," he shouted suddenly.

The squirrel cowered. "Oh no, sir," he whimpered. "I didn't eat any. I just—well, sort of pulled one up. To see how they grow. I—I'm interested in how things grow," he added.

"Indeed!" said Freddy. "Interested in how things grow, eh? I suppose you never thought how the onion feels about it—being pulled up by the roots, just so someone could see how it grows? Pretty callous, you are, for such a young one."

"And, oh boy, will Mr. Bean pull you up by the roots when he hears of this," put in Jinx.

"Unless, of course," said Freddy, "you had some good reason."

"Oh, I did," said the squirrel. "But I can't tell you. My mother—"

"I expect she got a note this morning," interrupted the pig. "From someone we don't talk about much. Eh? Was that it?"

"Oh, sir, then you know about it! Yes, she— But I mustn't tell anybody, mother says."

So they went to see the squirrel's mother. It

was as Freddy had suspected: she had received a demand from the Ignormus. One dozen large onions to be laid under the third tree from the left of the bridge, or he'd eat her family all up.

"This is serious," said Freddy. "The Ignormus (if there is an Ignormus) must have written at least a dozen such notes from the look of things. Tell you what we'll have to do. We'll hide under the bridge tonight and watch. He'll have to come for all these vegetables before they get wilted. Then if he's what I suspect: a small animal with white tail and whiskers, we'll pounce on him and capture him. And if he's really a big animal with horns and claws—"

"He'll pounce on us," said Jinx. "That's a swell idea, Freddy."

"We'll just stay hidden," said Freddy. "There's no danger—or not much. Come on, Jinx. You know there's none of the other animals that I can ask, the way they all feel about me now. Look, Jinx. I've done things for you. Remember the time your head got caught in the cream bottle, and I got you out before Mrs. Bean found you? Remember—"

"O.K., O.K.," said the cat. "You'll have me crying in a minute. I'll go. But I'm not going for old friendship's sake; I'm going because I know if there was very much danger you'd be eight miles from that bridge tonight. If I'm not braver than you, pig, I'll eat my own tail."

"I'd like to see you try it," said Freddy, who was always interested in such speculations. "You know, I wonder: if you started eating your own tail, and went right on eating—hind legs, body, fore legs—you'd finally eat up your own head, wouldn't you?"

"Try that one on the Ignormus," said Jinx. "Come on, we've got to get those carrots for Mrs. Winnick."

Ordinarily it would have been easy enough to steal a dozen carrots from the vegetable garden. But today there were so many thieves of various shapes and sizes frantically pulling up radishes and picking beans and peas that they kept getting into one another's way, and although they all pretended not to see one another, for a pig of Freddy's position and standing in the community to join openly in such wholesale robbery was out of the question.

"The Ignormus must have a tremendous appetite," he said.

"He must have written a lot of letters last night," said Jinx. "Guess I'll go up to the Big Woods and see if he doesn't want to hire me as his secretary. But this isn't getting us any carrots. Here, I'll fix it." And he jumped up on the wall and shouted: "Look out! Look out! Here comes Mr. Bean!"

There was a great squeaking and scampering, and in half a minute the vegetable garden was as empty of animal life as the Big Woods themselves. And Jinx and Freddy went in and pulled up a dozen prime carrots without anyone seeing them.

It was fairly late in the afternoon before they finally got them up through the woods and under the bridge. They had had to hide them in the grass until Freddy could bring a paper bag from his library to put them in, and on the way up to the woods they were stopped a dozen times by inquisitive friends who wanted to know what they were carrying. But they got them there at last, and then settled down in a clump of bushes a little way up the road where they could see who came for them.

They had been there about half an hour when they found they were both getting very sleepy.

"Ho, *hum*!" yawned Freddy. "We simply mustn't go to sleep, Jinx. We may have to wait here half the night, and it isn't even dark yet. How would it be," he said brightly, "if I was to recite some of my poetry to you?"

"You can try it," said the cat doubtfully. "But you know, to me poetry—well, it's like sitting in a car and watching the telegraph poles go by. The rhymes go by—heart, dart; love, dove—just like the poles. And I don't know what it is—they send me right off. Now if you had some poetry that didn't rhyme—"

"But then it wouldn't be poetry," Freddy objected.

"O.K.," said the cat. "I'm just telling you.

Goodness knows I'm no authority on poetry. I'm a great authority on sleep, though. Sleep; now that's my subject. I've studied it from every angle. Boy, how I've studied sleep! And you know, I feel a study period coming on right now." And he began to purr and closed his eyes.

"No, no," said Freddy. "We mustn't. Listen, Jinx; let me just recite the B verse from my alphabet poem. I'd like your opinion of it. You see, first I say: 'Bees, bothered by bold bears, behave badly.' And the verse goes like this.

> *"Your honey or your life!" says the bold*
>   *burglar bear,*
> *As he climbs up the tree where the bees have*
>   *their lair.*
> *"Burglars! Burglars!" The tree begins to*
>   *hum.*
>   *"Sharpen up your stings, brothers! Tight-*
>   *en up your wings, brothers!*
> *"Beat the alarm on the big bass drum!*

> *"Watch yourself, bear, for*
> > *here*
> > > *we*
> > > > *come!"*
>
> *Then the big black bees buzz out from their*
> > *lair.*
> *With sharp stings ready zoom down on the*
> > *bear.*
> *"Ouch! Ouch! Ouch! Don't be so rough!"*
> > *He slithers down the tree, squalling, "Hey,*
> > > *let me be!" Bawling*
> *"Keep your old honey. Horrid sticky stuff!*
> *"I'm going home, for*
> > > *I've*
> > > > *had*
> > > > > *enough!"*

Although he made many very appropriate
gestures when he recited, Freddy always tilted
his head back and shut his eyes. He said it
made him put more feeling into it. When he
had finished and opened his eyes, he saw that
the cat was sound asleep.

"Well of all the—" he began angrily, and

suddenly stopped, for he saw something moving down the road. He waked up Jinx quietly, and the two watched as a small grey animal came slowly along towards them, stopping every now and then to sniff the air suspiciously.

"By gum, it's Simon!" said the cat suddenly. With one leap he was out on the road, and before the rat could scuttle off into the bushes Jinx had him.

Simon knew better than to struggle. He knew that the sharp claws that were just barely pricking his back would dig deeper if he didn't lie still.

"Well, well," he said with a malicious smile, "my old friend the mouse-chaser! Quite a surprise! Turned hold-up man, now, eh? Molesting unprotected and innocent citizens on the public roads. Well, I'm not surprised. You always had the makings of a gangster in you, Jinx."

"Better be polite, rat," said Jinx, "or I'll tickle you. Like this." And he wiggled his claws gently.

The rat squirmed. "You let me alone," he

squeaked. "What right have you got to pick on me? This road isn't on old Bean's property. I'm going along minding my own business. You mind yours."

"Your business *is* our business, Simon, old shifty-eye," said Jinx.

"It's funny," said Freddy, "that I've only been up here a few times, and yet twice I've seen you on the road. Last time you'd been visiting your relatives in Iowa. What is it this time?"

But instead of answering, Simon burst into shrieks of hysterical laughter as he wriggled and twisted in the effort to get away from Jinx, who hadn't been able to resist the temptation to tickle him again.

"Let him alone, Jinx," said Freddy. "I want him to talk, not yell in that undignified way."

So when Jinx had released him, Simon sat up, and said: "I don't know why you've got any more right to ask me what I'm doing here than I have to ask you. However, since you're so interested, there is no reason why I shouldn't be perfectly frank."

"You let me alone," he squeaked.

"Oh-oh," said Jinx, "look out for a bigger one than usual."

Simon grinned maliciously at the cat. "I would scarcely expect *you* to believe me," he said. "People that tell lies all the time themselves don't know the truth when they hear it. But I will tell you, Freddy, that the reason you see me in this neighborhood again is that I am on my way to visit my son, Ezra, who lives over beyond Centerboro."

"You're a great family for visiting," said Jinx, "though why any of you ever want to see any of the others beats me. You aren't handsome, you aren't honest, you aren't even very good company—"

"Spare me your compliments," said Simon. "And if there's nothing else you want to know, will you allow me to continue my journey? It is getting dark, and personally I would like to be as far from the Big Woods before nightfall as possible. I haven't asked you what you are doing here, but I will tell you one thing you're doing: you're taking chances that I wouldn't care to take. However, I warned you before.

and if you choose to ignore my warning, it's you that will be clawed to pieces—not me. Good evening, gentlemen."

He spoke the last word so sarcastically that Jinx moved towards him again, but Freddy held the cat back. "Let him go," he said.

"But I want to tickle him again," the cat pleaded. "He makes such funny noises."

But Freddy wouldn't let him, and the rat scuttled off down the road.

"I don't like Simon being around here so much," said Freddy. "He may be telling the truth, of course. But if he and his family are planning to come back here to live, we're going to have more trouble on our hands."

"Well, they certainly aren't living anywhere around here now," said Jinx. "A family of rats can't live in a neighborhood without somebody seeing them, and nobody's seen anything of them except you, these two times on the road."

"I guess you're right," said the pig. "It's when they get settled in as they did in Mr. Bean's barn, with runways and passages and

front doors and back doors and secret en-
trances that they're hard to get rid of. And
we'd stop them doing that another time. Gosh,
we've got trouble enough with this Ignormus
(if there is an Ignormus), without having rats
around. Come on, let's get back in our hiding
place."

They found that after the encounter with
Simon they weren't sleepy any more, and they
watched the sun down and the moon up, and
they watched the moon swing across the sky
and follow the sun down, but still nothing
stirred, and no Ignormus came to call for the
carrots and other vegetables. At last about
three, in the morning Jinx got up and
stretched.

"Guess those notes were somebody's idea of
a joke," he said. "If the Ignormus was coming, he'd have come by this time."

"Whoever wrote those notes wrote the one
I found in the Grimby house," said Freddy.
"And that wasn't a joke. No sir; the Ignormus
(if there is an Ignormus) wrote them, and—"

"Why do you keep saying: *if* there is an Ignormus?" cut in Jinx irritably.

"Because I don't really believe there is."

"Yeah?" said the cat. "And so you come up here to watch all night for him! Well, if he doesn't exist, then we've seen him, we've seen what you expected to see, so let's go home." And he walked out of the hiding place.

Freddy followed more slowly. And suddenly both animals looked up at a slight noise in the treetops on the Big Woods side of the road, and then with a terrified yell leaped the ditch and dove into the underbrush. For floating down silently like an enormous owl was a great white shape that hovered over them and seemed about to drop and seize them. In a last horrified glance over their shoulders, they saw on the front end of the creature a sort of head, with what looked like two long white horns. And then they were galloping and stumbling and tripping and panting their way down through the woods to safety.

"So he doesn't exist, hey?" said Jinx, when

they had at last thrown themselves down on the grass by the brook and had caught their breath. "Or else he's a little animal with white whiskers. Huh! I suppose you'll tell me that was a shadow or a cloud, or maybe Hank learning to fly."

"No, it was *something*, all right," said Freddy.

"Something I don't have to get any better acquainted with," replied the cat. "Flying elephants are out of my line. I'm going home."

"Well, I'm not," said Freddy firmly. "Mr. Bean thinks I'm a thief, and all the animals are mad at me because I haven't done anything about the Ignormus (if there is—)" he stopped. "Well, it looks as if there was one, after all. Anyway, I'm not coming home until I've solved this case. Either," he said dramatically—"either I bring home the white hide of that Ignormus and nail it on the barn door, or you will never see your old Freddy again."

"Uh-huh," said Jinx, who was never much impressed by speeches of this kind. "Well, don't let him get your hide. And if you want help, you know where to find me. So long."

When Jinx had gone, Freddy sat and thought for a while. And this time he didn't go to sleep. Never, in any of his detective cases, had he met so many reverses, or been so baffled. And the animals were beginning to mistrust his ability. If he failed now he would never be Freddy, the great detective any more; he would be just Freddy—a pig. He got up and walked slowly in the growing light of dawn towards the Big Woods.

Chapter 12

For once Freddy had no plan of campaign. He was going into the Big Woods and find the Ignormus. He didn't know whether he'd talk to him, or fight with him, or run away. He didn't feel at all brave just determined, even though he was half scared to death. That is the best kind of bravery. It isn't any trick to be brave when you're not scared. And Freddy was scared all right. His tail had come completely uncurled. But he went on.

When he got to the road, he looked for the vegetables that the various animals had left for the Ignormus. And sure enough they were gone. Evidently he had collected them. Freddy crossed the road and plunged into the Big Woods. It was dark and it was scary, but Freddy trudged steadily along, and as he trudged he made up a little song to keep his spirits up. It went like this:

> *It was dark in the woods,*
> *It was very, very scary,*
> *But the pig trudged along,*
> *Always watchful and wary.*
> *The pig trudged along,*
> *And he made a little song*
> *(He was rather literary)*
> *It was quite extraordinary*
> *How he sang his little song*
> *In a voice clear and strong.*
> *Though it's rather customary*
> *For a pig, when something's wrong*
> *In a forest dark and scary,*
> *Dim and Dark and solitary.*

To sneak quietly along
Not to be so very, very
Brave and bold and military.

But this pig, he was bold,
He was brave as a lion,
And he walked through the woods
Without yellin' or cryin'—

Freddy had got to this place in his song, and was indeed feeling quite bold, when he gave a yell and leaped three feet in the air. Well, maybe he didn't leap three feet, but it was a good six inches. For something had jumped out of the underbrush at him.

The something was only Theodore, as Freddy fortunately saw before he could gather his legs under him and start to run. The frog sat up on his hind legs and saluted. "Your faithful hound, sir," he said.

"Nothing very faithful about scaring me to death," Freddy grumbled.

"I could have scared you worse by staying in the bushes and giving little gug-gug—I mean grunts. I just thought if you were going up for that g-gun I'd like to go along."

"Come on, then," said Freddy. "Only stop stammering, will you? Now I know why you do it, I know you're just taking time to think up smart things to say, and I'm not in the mood for smart conversation."

So they went on up towards the Grimby house. Nothing happened until they got within sight of the house. Then they stopped.

"The front door's closed," said Freddy.

"It was open last time we were here," said Theodore.

Freddy took a deep breath, and his tail, which had been uncurled because he was scared, was now curled up tight with determination. "Come on," he said between his teeth, and started on towards the house.

But this time Theodore didn't follow him. "There's something sticking out of the window beside the door," said the frog. "And whenever we move, it moves too and keeps pointing at us."

Freddy kept on a step or two, and then

stopped again, for he had seen the thing too. He moved to the right, and the thing moved to the right and pointed at him. Then he jumped to the left, and it swung over to the left, still pointing. "Funny," he said. "I can't imagine—" And then he said: "Oh, gosh!" and ducked quickly back among the trees. For he had seen two holes in the end of the thing, and he realized all at once that it was Mr. Bean's shotgun.

Now a double-barreled shotgun holds two cartridges, and has two triggers, one for each barrel. For the life of him Freddy couldn't remember whether, when he had shot the gun off, he had pulled both triggers, or only one. If he'd pulled both, why the gun was as harmless as a stick, because there weren't any extra cartridges. But if he'd pulled only one, then there was still a cartridge in the other barrel, and the Ignormus, or whoever was pointing the gun at him, could easily pull that other trigger and the results would be unpleasant.

He explained all this to Theodore, but the frog seemed to feel that there wasn't much danger. "Oh, go on, Freddy," he said. "You said you were going into the house, no matter what. You were going to beard the Ignormus in his lair, you said."

"Oh, I said, I said!" replied Freddy crossly. "I didn't say I was going to walk right up and let somebody shoot me."

"He can't shoot you if there isn't anything in the gun. And if it is still loaded, he'd probably pull the wrong trigger. And if he pulled the right trigger, the chances are he isn't a very good shot and he'd miss you. And if he did hit you—"

"Look, frog," interrupted Freddy. "I'm not *going*. So stop arguing. I've got an idea, anyway. I'm going to get Randolph."

So they started back. It was funny, Freddy thought as he trotted along, how you always walked very slowly when you went into the Big Woods, but going out again you almost ran. Theodore, for instance, had taken just little hops on the way in, but now he was clearing the ground in great leaps that soon sent him out of sight ahead. "I guess," Freddy thought, "if you were scared all the time, you'd get a lot more work done." And he was trying to think out a scheme for scaring people that worked in factories and shops, so that they'd get all their day's work done in the morning, and would have the afternoon free to play games, when Theodore came sailing back over a bush and landed at his feet. "Sssssh," whispered the frog. "There's something going on out in the road. Sneak up quietly."

So they worked their way silently along from tree to tree until they could see the road, just where it ran over the little bridge. Behind one of the uprights that held up the bridge railing an animal was crouching. He was small, but he was one of the queerest animals anybody ever saw. For his tail seemed to be a plume of feathers, and his whiskers—well, they were the kind of whiskers you seldom see on an animal; in fact, you seldom see them anywhere. I have never seen them except on Mr. Bean, whose whiskers were thick and bushy, and covered his face right up to the eyes. This animal's whiskers might have been modeled on Mr. Bean's, for his face was just a fluff of white, above which a pair of beady black eyes peered suspiciously.

"That was the animal that was around the bank the morning after the robbery," whispered Freddy. "Something familiar about those eyes, too," he added. "Seems as though there was. Well, what kind of animal do you call him, Theodore?"

"If a feather duster had four legs and got married to a powder puff," said the frog, "I expect their children would look like that. Gosh, is this thing the Ignormus?"

Freddy didn't answer, because just then a young hen came timidly out of the bushes on the other side of the road. Around her neck was a little basket in which were some eggs. She put the basket down on the grass at one side of the bridge, and having pulled her head back through the basket handle, was turning to run into the woods again when the bushes were pushed aside and Charles stepped out and confronted her.

"Just a moment, Chirpita," he said sternly. "You thought you had given your old father the slip, didn't you? Well, I saw you making off with those eggs this morning, and so I followed you. Sneaking out of the henhouse so cleverly! You thought you were pretty smart, didn't you? But you're not as smart as your old father; not yet, you aren't. I knew where you were off to. Meeting that young rooster from over the hill again, eh? That good-for-nothing young idler! I tell you, Chirpita, I will not have it—I will not allow you to have anything to do with that wretch, that whippersnapper, that beetle-brained young imbecile."

"He's not, either!" sobbed Chirpita angrily. "Anyway, mother thinks he's all right."

"Your mother is a very fine hen," said Charles with dignity. "But with all due respect to her many superior qualities, she does not know people as I do. She does not look beneath the glitter of surface appearances. *I* sized up that young fellow the moment I saw him. A lot of feathers and a strut: that's all there is to him. And when you marry, my girl,

"Stop!" he called.

you're going to marry something more than that. Now pick up that basket and come home with me."

"But father, I *didn't* come out here to meet Benjy," she said. "I came because I—well, mother knows about it. But I wasn't to tell you or anyone."

"Ha!" said Charles. "I believe you. But your father is cleverer than he looks—"

"Oh yes, father," she interrupted. "Mother always tells us that."

"What!" Charles demanded. "What do you mean by that?" And then, apparently deciding that no answer would be very pleasant to such a question, he said: "Come; we'll talk this over with your mother."

But as the hen stooped to put her head through the basket handle, the animal on the bridge stepped out into view. "Stop!" he called. "Those eggs are the property of the Ignormus. Remove them at your peril!"

Charles turned and looked him arrogantly up and down. "Well, upon my soul!" he said. "Where'd you come from? Escaped from some circus, I suppose. On your way, friend," he added, with a wave of his claw.

But Chirpita said: "It's true, father; he's right. I guess I'd better tell you. Mother found a note from the Ignormus this morning, saying we'd have to bring half a dozen eggs up here, or he'd come and eat us up. I—I guess we'd better leave them."

"I guess you better had," said the strange animal. "Don't interfere with the Ignormus, rooster, or you'll be nothing but a handful of feathers blowing around the woods by night."

"Oh," said Charles weakly. "Well . . . in that case. . . ." He stopped. Then he looked at the animal again and said: "But you—you are not the Ignormus, are you, sir?"

"I'm his butler," said the animal.

"But I thought the Ig—the . . . excuse me, but I don't like to say his name. I thought he lived all alone."

"He did," replied the other. "For many years he lived alone. But he got tired of waiting on himself and cooking his own meals and making his own bed, and so on. He thought of hiring servants, but he was so terrible looking that he couldn't get anybody to work for him. All the animals just ran away screaming when they first saw him. So then he heard about me and my family, and he sent to Africa for us. We're the only animals in the world that aren't frightened of anything. We're practically unscareable."

"Indeed," said Charles politely. "And may I ask—oh, we'll leave the eggs, but may I ask—what kind of animals you are?"

"You may ask," said the animal, "but I don't have to answer, and I'm not going to. We've waited too long as it is, and the Ignormus is already up and calling for his breakfast. So if you'll just leave those eggs and go about your business—"

Freddy and Theodore had seen and heard everything that went on. Freddy would have liked to capture the strange animal, but he felt sure that the creature would get away before he could get to him. And then he had a bright idea. He remembered how furious Charles had been at the truck driver, and at Jinx, when they had called him a chicken, and so just as the animal finished speaking, Freddy mimicked his voice, and said: "You big chicken, you!"

Charles swung around quickly. His feathers, which had been drooping more and more, were suddenly fluffed out, and there was fire in his eye. "What did you say?" he demanded.

The animal, hearing a voice behind him, had glanced over his shoulder, but now turned back to Charles. "I said to go about your business," he repeated.

"You big chicken, you!" repeated Freddy from his hiding place.

Charles strutted up on to the bridge. "Just say that again," he demanded. "Just say that again."

"What's the matter with you?" said the animal. "I didn't say anything but to put the eggs down."

"You big chicken, you!" repeated Freddy, again.

"Now look here, my friend," said Charles menacingly. "You've called me a chicken once too often. Put up your paws, you unscareable white-whiskered imitation of a stuffed monstrosity." And he spread his wings and lowered his beak.

"But I didn't call you anything," protested the other. "It was someone over in the woods. I heard them—"

"Oh, yes? And who'd be in the Big Woods? Put 'em up, white-tail. I'm coming in." And he flew at the animal.

Freddy and Theodore were so amazed at the ferocity of Charles's attack that for nearly a minute they didn't move. Freddy was almost as goggle-eyed as the frog. The battle raged back and forth across the bridge, and the air was full of white fluff and feathers, for although the unscareable animal was putting up a good fight, his teeth were no match for Charles's beak and claws, and his tail and whiskers were rapidly being converted into a very good imitation of a snowstorm. And then, before Freddy could collect himself and come to Charles's assistance, it was all over, the animal was lying on his back with one of Charles's claws on his neck, and as Freddy came rushing out, the rooster flapped his wings and gave a loud, if rather breathless, crow.

And then Freddy got the surprise of his life. For as he looked down at the defeated animal who was panting and snarling weakly, and saw him stripped of his white whiskers and tail feathers, he recognized him. "Why it's Ezra!" he exclaimed. "All disguised with feathers held to his tail with a rubber band, and cotton whiskers that he holds in his mouth. My goodness, Charles, I'd never have thought you could lick a rat. They're terrible fighters."

"Pooh," said Charles. "That's nothing. You've always underrated me, Freddy. You and all the other animals. But I guess that shows you. I guess nobody'll say again that—" He stopped suddenly, as the real meaning of what Freddy had said dawned on him. "A rat!" he exclaimed, and took his claw quickly off Ezra's neck. And even though he had won the fight, he looked confused and a little scared, for no rooster in his right mind will tackle a rat. "Really," he said backing away,

"I didn't realize—I had no idea—"

If there had been any fight left in Ezra he could have got up then and given Charles a good beating. But he had had enough. "Aw, shut up!" he said weakly, and closed his eyes.

Freddy bent over him. "I might have known," he said, "with Simon around, that the rest of his family wouldn't be far off. But where you've all been beats me. You can't have been living in the Big Woods, and—"

"Who says we can't?" snarled Ezra. "We work for the Ignormus, just as I told you. And —oh, boy!—when he hears of this, what he'll do to you, rooster, will be plenty!"

"Well, really," said Charles apologetically, "if I'd known—"

"Keep still, Charles," interrupted Freddy. "You licked Ezra in a fair fight. Don't go backing down now. Besides, I don't believe there's any Ignormus. I think that Simon and his gang are at the bottom of all these robberies. Probably they have a secret hideout up here somewhere—for they wouldn't dare try to live in the Big Woods—"

"Oh, wouldn't we!" broke in Ezra. "And you don't believe there's any Ignormus, hey? What did you run for, then, when he started down out of the trees after you last night?"

"Well," said Freddy doubtfully, "he didn't hurt me much. But suppose there is an Ignormus, and that you work for him, as you say. —Why, of course," he exclaimed; "that handwriting on the letters was yours, Ezra. I remember when I taught you to write, you always made your d's with a funny tail. I wondered where I'd seen them before. You wrote those intimidating letters."

"Sure, I did," replied the rat boldly. "The boss—the Ignormus—I mean—he writes a beautiful hand, but the trouble is, it's such beautiful writing nobody can read it. So when he wants to write letters that the people he sends 'em to are supposed to read, I write 'em for him."

"All letters are supposed to be read," said Freddy.

"No they aren't either. Not the Ignormus's. Suppose he wants to write a letter to scare some animal. He writes it in his beautiful hand, and signs it 'The Ignormus.' The animal gets it, and tries to read it, and can't. 'Oh, dear,' he says; 'what *now?*' He's sure the letter contains a threat, but he can't find out what it is, and he becomes scareder and scareder. Whereas if I'd written the letter for the Ignormus, and said: 'I'm going to eat you up at five o'clock on Friday,' the animal would just have hidden at five on Friday, and wouldn't be half so scared. It's the same way when he thanks people for Christmas presents. Suppose you give him some slippers for Christmas. He writes a 'thank you' letter, but you can't read it. You aren't sure whether he liked the slippers or not. So next year you spend more money on him, so as to be sure to send him something he'll like better than the slippers."

"I see," said Freddy. "If he just had you write: 'Thank you for the beautiful slippers,' why next year maybe I'd think I wouldn't have to send him anything more than a Christmas card. His letters are sort of like Charles's speeches: they look lovely until you try to find

out what they mean. Well, Ezra, I guess we'll
take you down to the farm and lock you up.
Let me see, there's an old parrot cage up in
the loft that will do fine. But first I want you to
answer some questions. Was it you and your
family that robbed the bank?"

Ezra was beginning to feel better. He sat
up, felt gingerly of one or two sore spots,
twirled his whiskers with one paw, and with a
sly look at Freddy, said: "Sure. We did it, and
the Ignormus stood guard. He sat on the bank
and watched us dig. I guess that bank is pretty
solidly built, or he'd have squashed it flat. You
know what the boss weighs? Two thousand
eight hundred and seventy-four pounds. And
he's been dieting, too. But now with all the
animals bringing him good will offerings of
vegetables and so on, and with occasional frogs
and roosters, and maybe a pig on Sunday, I
expect he'll soon plump out again. —Why
there he is now!" he exclaimed, jumping up
and staring into the woods and waving his
arms. "Hey, boss!" he shouted.

The others turned and stared in the same

direction. But there was nothing there—nothing but the great motionless tree trunks, and the millions of green leaves. And when they turned to look at Ezra again, there was nothing there either. For the rat had sneaked quietly away.

Chapter 13

The three friends trudged disconsolately homeward—at least, Freddy and Charles trudged; Theodore hopped, as usual. They were pretty mad at having been taken in by such an old trick. Freddy had even tried to kick himself for not keeping a sharper eye on Ezra, but it isn't easy to kick yourself, and if you are a pig it is practically impossible. He only succeeded in kicking Charles, which didn't add to the happiness of the occasion.

At the pool in the woods, Theodore said

good-bye, and with a leap and a plop he was gone. Charles gazed at the widening ripples on the pool's surface. "Thus friends depart," he said mournfully; "here one moment, gone the next. And here I stand, alone, bereft—"

"Oh, shut up, Charles," said Freddy. "You've just licked a rat in fair fight. What are you kicking about? It's something I bet no rooster has ever done before. If anybody's bereft, it's me. Mr. Bean mad at me, everybody saying I'm a no good detective, it seems sometimes as if every animal's paw was against me. By the way, what does 'bereft' mean?"

"Goodness, you ought to know," said the rooster. "It's a regular poet's word; that's why I used it. I thought you'd understand it."

"Yeah," said Freddy. "But what does it mean?"

"Well it—it—Oh, what does it matter what it means? You always want everything *explained.* I use a nice word, a fine word, a word that would be a bright jewel in any poem, and instead of just looking at it and saying: 'That's

a darn fine word,' you want to define it. You—"
He broke off suddenly. They had walked
along as they talked, and had come out of the
woods into the meadow beside the brook.
"What's going on here?"

The meadow, which had recently been
mowed, was dotted with little groups of small
animals, all moving steadily in one direction.
There were rabbits and squirrels and chip-
munks, woodchucks and mice, and nearly all
of them carried something in their mouths:
bulging paper bags, or bundles done up in bits
of old rag. At the far end of the field, Freddy
saw his young cousin, Weedly, who seemed to
be having a heated argument with a family
of skunks.

The skunk who was doing most of the talking Freddy recognized as his friend, Sniffy
Wilson, and he ran across to him.

"What's it all about?" he asked. "Where
you off to, Sniffy?"

"They're running away," said Weedly indignantly. "Deserting the farm. Look,

Freddy; all the animals are leaving and taking their household belongings with them. Isn't it awful?"

"It may be awful," said Sniffy, "but it's awfuller to stay here. With Mr. Bean mad at all the animals, and threatening to shoot us on sight—though how he's to shoot, when his gun's been stolen, I don't know. And with this terrible Ignormus roaming all over the farm all night, stealing things and pouncing on everything that moves. Why, this used to be as safe as Centerboro Main Street on Sunday afternoon, this farm. But now our wives and children hardly dare stick their noses outdoors even in broad daylight. And with these new robberies last night—"

"What robberies?" Freddy asked. "I was up in the woods all night. Has something else happened?"

So between them, Weedly and Sniffy told him what had happened. It was plenty. The oat bin in the barn had been raided again, and another attempt had been made to rob the bank, but this latter had been foiled by the mouse on guard, who had rung the alarm bell. All the animals had turned out and had hunted several hours for the robbers, but hadn't found any sign of them. When some of them got home, however, they found that in their absence their pantries had been broken into, and food taken. Moreover, when the two dogs and the two cats had gone off to answer the alarm bell, someone or something had got into the house and taken a bag of butternuts from the pantry. This was pretty serious, for these butternuts were a Christmas present for Mr. Bean from some of the woods animals, and he had been saving them so that Mrs. Bean could put them in a cake for his birthday. He'd be pretty mad when he knew they'd been stolen.

"Oh, dear," said Freddy gloomily, "I suppose he'll suspect me of that, too. I'll be as popular around this farm as a—" He had been going to say "skunk," but then he remembered that he was talking to Sniffy, so he stopped.

Sniffy didn't seem to notice it. He was a nice

fellow, but not very sensitive. "Better come along with us," he said. "I thought we'd pick out a nice farm down on the Flats, and settle there. Of course I know you're fond of the Beans, but with things as they are now—"

"Don't talk nonsense!" said Freddy sharply. "With things as they are now, it's just the time when we shouldn't leave. Maybe Mr. Bean *is* mad at me, but I'm not mad at him. And it seems to me that to desert him now, when things are going wrong, is a pretty mean trick. Indeed, I feel," he went on in a louder voice, as some of the other refugees came crowding up to hear what was going on, "that as citizens of the First Animal Republic, the only free animal republic in the world, we will, if we leave now, be deserting under fire."

There was a murmur of applause, and Sniffy said: "Gosh, I hadn't thought about it that way."

Freddy was going on to say more, but Charles, who had now come up, saw a chance of making a speech, and as that was a chance he never missed if he could help it, he fluttered up to the top rail of the fence and held up one claw for silence.

"Friends and fellow citizens," he shouted, "you have heard what Freddy has said. I wish to endorse his statements with the full power of my well known eloquence. As citizens of the great free commonwealth of the F.A.R., under whose shining banner we have for so long enjoyed the fruits of peace, I call upon you now to band together to rid our country of the oppressor, to free it from the bonds of the tyrant. By what right do I thus call upon you, you ask. By the right of one, I reply, who though but a lowly rooster, has this day defeated in fair fight one of that tyrant's ferocious henchmen. Yes I, your old friend Charles, have fought and beaten, for the glory of Mr. Bean and the honor of the F.A.R., the Ignormus's servant, Ezra."

A buzz of excitement ran among the listeners, and they all looked inquiringly at Freddy, who nodded assurance of the truth of the rooster's boast.

For a while, as other animals came running

over from the barnyard, Charles went on praising himself, and describing the fight in detail. But Freddy interrupted him. "Never mind the fight, Charles," he said. "Give 'em the patriotic stuff. They must stick to Mr. Bean."

So Charles continued. "But my friends, enough of my modest exploit. What of you, my compatriots? What of Mr. Bean? What of our glorious republic? Are they to go down to ruin under the onslaughts of our cruel enemies, the Ignormus and his accomplices, Simon and his gang? I say to you: No, a thousand times, no! Let us band together, let us close up our ranks, resolved to do or die, and advance upon the enemy. What do you say, animals? Are we afraid of the Ignormus?"

He paused for a reply, but for a moment there was none. Then a small rabbit in the front row said: "Yes."

"That's the wrong answer," said Charles, looking down at him severely.

Many of the others, however, seemed to agree with the rabbit. But Freddy went up to the fence and turned to face the crowd, which by this time included most of the animals on the farm.

"What our young friend has said is right," he declared. "We *are* afraid of the Ignormus. I am; you are; even my gallant friend Charles is, though he quite rightly hates to admit it."

"I am not!" said Charles crossly.

"But," continued Freddy, "the greatest bravery is found in those who go ahead, even though they *are* afraid. That, animals, is what we must do. We must show this superior bravery; we must defend the honor of Bean; we must drive the Ignormus and his confederates from their lair; we must make the Big Woods safe for the smallest and weakest animal who wishes to walk there."

A wave of enthusiasm swept over the audience, and they cheered and cheered. Freddy's eloquence had rather carried him away; he had had no intention of starting a crusade against the Ignormus—at least, not yet. But he saw at once that the martial spirit must not be allowed to die down without action. If he did not lead the animals now against the enemy, he would never have another chance. For if he put it off, even for a day, they would become frightened again, and then they would leave the farm, by ones and twos and families. They would migrate from the Bean farm, just as at some time in the past they had migrated from the Big Woods. And they would never come back.

Freddy had started something, and he wasn't at all sure that he could finish it. He thought of the enormous white shape that had floated down towards them in the darkness, and he shivered. He thought of that shotgun pointing at him from the window of the Grimby house, and he shuddered. He thought of the big family of Simon's kin, lurking under the Ignormus's protection in the gloom of the Big Woods, and he shook.

But then he pulled himself together. These animals, no one of whom would have stepped a foot inside the Big Woods an hour ago; many of whom were even leaving their homes for fear of the Ignormus,—they would follow him right up to the door of the Grimby house. Their fighting spirit was aroused; they were in a mood to tackle twenty Ignormuses. Some in the crowd had already raised the Marching Song of the F.A.R.

Freddy pushed through the crowd to where Mrs. Wiggins was standing. "Look here," he said quickly; "I can't hold this crowd much longer. You take charge, as President of the F.A.R., will you? I've got an idea, and I've got to carry it out before this mob starts for the Big Woods. Can't explain now. I need a couple of hours. You can use it in getting them organized into companies, with captains and so on, and getting out the flag, and generally whooping up their spirits. Will you?"

"My land, Freddy," said the cow, "I'll try. I wish I'd had some experience in the army. I'm no general."

"You are now," said the pig. "General Wiggins, and don't you forget it. This is our chance to lick the Ignormus, and we've got to take it. Give me two hours, and then lead your army into the Big Woods and surround the

Grimby house. I'll be there, and we'll decide on a plan of attack then."

He dashed off up the brook. At the third stone above the apple tree on the left side of the brook, he stopped and rapped sharply with a fore trotter. At once an elderly, rather motherly looking beetle came out from under the stone. When she saw him, she said, "Good morning," and dropped a curtsey. At least she tried to, but her legs got tangled up and she sat down heavily.

"Drat it!" she said. "I never can manage that properly."

"Where's Randolph?" Freddy asked.

"Eh?" said the beetle, putting one foot up behind her ear.

Freddy repeated the question in a louder tone.

"Well, no," said the beetle. "I don't think it will rain before tomorrow."

Freddy put his snout down close to her and yelled: "Where's Randolph?" at the top of his lungs.

"You don't need to bellow like that," she

"Eh?" said the beetle.

said mildly. "I'm only a mite deef. You want Randy, eh? He's round here somewhere, by the brook, hunting mosquito eggs. Never saw such a boy for mosquito eggs. I tell him so many of them aren't good for him, but will he listen to me? I guess not!" She droned on her mild complaints about her son.

"Oh, dear!" said Freddy, and he was turning disconsolately away when something black came swiftly through the grass stems and stopped before him.

"Randolph!" exclaimed Freddy. "Thank goodness! Look, Randolph, you said if I needed your help to come for you, and I do need it very badly. I think I'm not saying too much if I say that the fate of the Bean farm, at least as far as the animals are concerned, rests with you."

"H'm," said the beetle shortly; "pretty big responsibility for a bug. However. Do what I can. You taught me to handle my legs. Guess I can do something for you. Command me."

"Well," said Freddy, "I want you to come up to the Big Woods and do some scouting for me. And maybe some gnawing. You've got good strong jaws, haven't you?"

"Cut anything but tin," said Randolph.

"Good," said the pig. "Climb up on my back. We haven't much time." And when Randolph had climbed up Freddy's leg—which took some time, for it tickled a good deal and Freddy couldn't help squirming—away they went.

This time Freddy didn't try to go quietly when he got into the Big Woods. He plunged along through the underbrush, taking care not to let the beetle get swept off, and didn't stop until he reached the place from which he and Theodore had seen the gun pointing from the window of the Grimby house. Sure enough, there it was, and as it swung around to cover him, he squatted down behind a tree and gave Randolph his instructions.

The beetle slipped down from Freddy's back and started towards the house. He advanced in short rushes from one clump of grass to the next, like a skirmisher creeping up on the enemy. He reached the porch, climbed it, made a dash across without being noticed, and walked up the wall under the window. In another second or two he was walking down the under side of the gun barrel towards the muzzle.

Freddy had instructed him to walk down the under side, because if someone was aiming the gun—and someone certainly was—that some-one would be squinting down the upper side of the barrel and would notice the beetle and probably shake him off. And then Freddy gave a groan. For Randolph slipped and fell to the porch floor. The steel gun barrel was too smooth.

Randolph didn't try to climb again. He went down off the porch, and Freddy, who had pretty keen eyes, saw that he was chewing up a dandelion stalk and rubbing his six feet in the juice.

"By gum, that's clever, " said the pig to him-self. "Making his feet stick."

This time Randolph walked right down to the muzzle of the gun and disappeared inside one barrel. After a minute he came out and disappeared inside the other one. Then he came out again, dropped to the porch, and in a few minutes was back beside the pig.

"Guess only one cartridge has been fired," he said. "Right hand barrel smells of powder smoke, and the cartridge shell is empty. Left hand barrel is clean, and the cartridge shell has a little cardboard cap or stopper on it, as you told me."

"Do you think you could gnaw through the cardboard?" Freddy asked.

"Give me five minutes alone with it," said the beetle, "and you can drive a team of caterpillars through it."

"Well, you see," said the pig, "that cap holds the shot in. If you can gnaw through it, and then we can get him to tip the gun barrel down, all the shot will run right out. Then if he shoots at me it won't make any difference, because he'll be shooting a blank cartridge."

"Leave it to me," said the beetle, and started off again.

In spite of his boast, it took Randolph a good quarter of an hour to gnaw through the cartridge cap. Freddy watched impatiently, but at last he saw one or two small round shot drop out of the barrel, then the beetle, who had evidently been pushing them along ahead of him, appeared, and a few minutes later he and Freddy were trying to think of some way to get whoever was aiming the gun to point the barrel down, so the shot would roll out. For the ground in front of the house where Freddy was hiding, was higher than the house itself, so that the gun was pointing a little upward.

"I could go in and roll 'em out, one by one," said Randolph. "But there's an awful lot of them."

Freddy shook his head. "The other animals would get here before you'd finished, and some of them might get shot."

"Maybe they'll get scared again, and won't come at all," said the beetle. "Fine speeches you and Charles made. Heard 'em over by the brook. Don't know when I've heard more stirring ones. But when they get all through cheering and begin to calm down—begin to think about that Ignormus with his terrible claws—"

"I guess you, being a bug, maybe don't understand us animals very well," said Freddy. "We've always known about the Ignormus, but he didn't bother us and we didn't bother him. Folks say rabbits who got too near the Big Woods disappeared, and maybe it's so. I never knew any of them personally."

"Too many of 'em anyway," said Randolph. "What's a rabbit or two?"

"Anyhow," continued the pig, "we kept away from the Big Woods and didn't worry. Sure, we kept away because we were afraid. You couldn't have dragged any animal on our farm up here with ropes. But while one animal might be afraid, by himself, a crowd of animals will tackle anything, once they get good and mad. They love their homes, and they love the farm, and the Beans. They don't want to leave here, and they don't want to see Mr. Bean robbed right and left. They're mad clear through. But I guess it didn't occur to them that they could do anything about it until Charles and I talked to them. Oh, they'll come all right."

Freddy was squatting down behind the tree, with the tip of his snout almost touching the beetle, for they were talking in whispers so as not to be heard in the house. There was a faint rustle in the grass, and turning his head Freddy saw a large centipede hurrying towards them.

"Why, Jeffrey!" exclaimed the beetle. "What you doing so far from home?"

"Hi, Randy," said the newcomer, and he reared up and looked suspiciously at the pig. "This guy bothering you?" he asked. "Want me to give him a nip?"

"No, no," said Randolph hastily. "He's my good friend, Freddy. Freddy, meet Jeffrey."

"Pleased, I'm sure," said the centipede. "Just came up to call on my cousins. They live in a stump up here a piece. But what are you doing here? Mosquito eggs?" He turned to the pig. "No accounting for tastes, eh, mister? I wouldn't touch mosquito eggs if I starved first. But Randy, here—I've seen him eat twenty-five at a sitting. And boy, how the mosquitoes hate him! Lucky you've got a hard shell, Randy, my boy. But what's going on?"

Randolph explained. When he had finished, Jeffrey said: "Let's have a look," and went rippling over towards the house. When he had looked at the gun, he came back. "Leave it to me," he said. "I can fix you up." And he went back the way he had come.

"Gosh, what can *he* do?" said Freddy disconsolately.

"Dunno," said the beetle. "But when he knows what he's doing, he don't waste words, Jeffrey don't. He's got something up his sleeve, all right."

"He hasn't got any sleeves," said Freddy peevishly.

"Well then," said Randolph, "*you* think of something."

Of course Freddy couldn't, so he didn't say any more. And after a few minutes, back came Jeffrey, and behind him were his cousins, twelve of them. They didn't stop. "Leave it to us," said Jeffrey as they headed for the house, their dozens of legs carrying them over the ground faster than a mouse can walk. They climbed the porch, rippled up the wall and down the under side of the gun barrel, and one by one disappeared into the muzzle. Presently, one by one, the round gleaming shot began dripping out of the muzzle on to the porch floor.

"Now, how in the world—?" said Freddy.

"Lying on their backs," said Randolph. "End to end. Passing the shot out with their feet. They sort of walk 'em out, upside down, if you see what I mean."

It didn't take more than a minute. Then the centipedes filed out, down the gun barrel, the wall, the porch, and came over to report.

"Not a shot left in the cartridge," said Jeffrey. "There was some black stuff back of the shot. Want us to get that out too?"

"That's gunpowder," said Freddy. "If you got careless it might go off."

"Here today and gone tomorrow," said Jeffrey. "If you say so we'll get it."

But Freddy said no, it wasn't necessary.

"O K," said Jeffrey. "Be seeing you." And the centipedes filed off without another word.

"I'd like to have thanked your friend," said Freddy. "He doesn't realize how great a service he has performed."

"He doesn't care," said Randolph. "If you'd thanked him, you'd just have embarrassed him. That's a centipede for you. Generous as all get out, but pretty hard-boiled."

"Yes, he didn't seem very sensitive," said Freddy. "Well, now I suppose we wait for the animals."

"If they come," said Randolph cynically.

Chapter 14

Down in the barnyard Mrs. Wiggins was mustering her troops. She had been President of the F.A.R. for so long that she had got used to being in authority and giving orders, and she was a much better general than you'd expect a cow to be. The smaller animals were divided into companies of twenty, each under a leader of their own choice. Of course they couldn't be expected to do much fighting against a creature like the Ignormus, or even against rats, but they could do a lot of shouting and running around, which is a large part of any battle anyway, and they could also be used as scouts. The center of the advance would be led by Mrs. Wiggins in person, supported by Robert, Georgie, Jinx and Minx. In recognition of his recent gallantry, Charles was assigned to command of the left wing, and under him were Henrietta, with several of their more robust children, Weedly, and a fox named John, who spent his summers on the farm. The right wing, commanded by Peter, the bear, was made up of Mrs. Wurzburger, Mrs. Wogus, Sniffy Wilson and his family, Bill, the goat, and a porcupine named Cecil.

Mrs. Wiggins had gone into the barn to get the flag of the F.A.R., which of course would be carried in the advance, when Mr. Bean drove into the yard. He had been to Centerboro to buy some traps to put in the vegetable garden, although he said he didn't know what good they would do now: there were so few vegetables that hadn't been stolen. When he saw the animals lined up in the barnyard, he hooked the reins around the whip socket and jumped out of the buggy.

Mrs. Bean had come to the kitchen door
and was watching.

"What in tarnation is going on here?" he
demanded, walking out in front of the army
and looking them over as he puffed furiously
at his pipe.

The animals looked at one another, but
didn't dare say anything. And just then Mrs.
Wiggins came out of the barn with the flag in
her mouth.

"Humph!" said Mr. Bean. "Another of your
parades, hey? Tomfoolery, I call it! Why
don't you get busy and stop this thieving that's
going on? Instead of giving parties." He
looked around. "Ain't the pig here? Freddy?
Humph! Run away, I suppose. Good rid-
dance, too. I don't like animals that steal
things." He clasped his hands behind him and
took a turn up and down with his eyes on the
ground. Then he lifted his head. "Why don't
you *ask,*" he shouted, "if you want things?
Oats, vegetables. Have I ever grudged you
anything? I—I—" He stopped, glared, then

turned to Mrs. Bean. "You tell 'em, Mrs. B.," he said.

Mrs. Bean came down off the kitchen porch. She was a round, apple-cheeked little woman, with snapping black eyes. All the animals were very fond of her.

"Mr. Bean only wants to say," she said quietly, "that he's always been very fond of all of you. You've done a great deal for him, and he appreciates it. You can have about anything on this farm that you want. And so he doesn't understand why you—some of you, that is— want to steal things from him. Is that about it, Mr. B.?"

"That's it exactly," said Mr. Bean. "And all this marching and flag-waving—"

"Oh, yes," said Mrs. Bean. "He doesn't think that this is any time for parading around, as if everything was all right."

This was too much for Mrs. Wiggins. She dropped the flag from her mouth and said: "We don't think everything is all right. And this isn't a parade: it's an army. We're going out to fight the robbers, and defeat them, and make them give back what they've stolen."

Mr. Bean didn't look at Mrs. Wiggins when she spoke. It always embarrassed him to hear an animal talk. I don't know why, but it did. But he stopped puffing his pipe so he could hear her. And Mrs. Bean said: "You know who the robbers are?"

"Yes, ma'am," said the cow. "It's a long story, and I haven't time to tell you now. But if Mr. Bean would only trust us for a little while—"

Mr. Bean didn't say anything, but he stopped puffing on his pipe so long that it went out, and that shows you how deeply he was affected. The only time I can ever remember that he stopped puffing so long that it went out before was when Mrs. Wiggins's grandmother broke her leg, and that was way back in 1903. He stood thinking for a minute; then he said to Mrs. Bean: "Guess Hank'll want to go along." And he went over and unharnessed Hank from the buggy.

Now Hank hadn't heard the stirring speeches of Charles and Freddy, and he didn't

"Yes, ma'am," said the cow.

know any more about what had been going on
than Mr. Bean did, because he had been in
Centerboro. And as the Beans walked back
and got up on the porch to watch the army
march away, he said to Mrs. Wiggins: "What's
this all about?"

"War," said Mrs. Wiggins grimly. "No time
to tell you now; I've got to get this army under
way. But Freddy's found out that the rats are
living in the Big Woods. They've made some
kind of an alliance with the Ignormus, and
that's what's behind all this robbing and plun-
dering. So we're going to clean them out.
You'd better carry the flag, Hank. We can
stick it through your halter."

"Oh, I dunno," said Hank doubtfully. "If
it's war—well, I've never attended any wars,
and I don't expect I'd be much good. Fighting,
I suppose?"

"Who ever heard of a war without fighting?" said the cow.

"I was afraid of that," said Hank. "Oh, I
guess you'd better count me out. I never did
like fighting—noisy, uncomfortable thing to

do. 'Tain't that I'm afraid, you understand—
at least I guess I'm not. Or am I? Well, maybe
I am, a mite. I ain't any hero, and that's what
you need for wars and such. I'm just an old
horse that wants to be comfortable and—"

"You're a worse talker than Charles, when
you get started," interrupted Mrs. Wiggins.
"Anyhow, you're going, so pick up that flag.
As for being afraid, you aren't any scareder
than I am, and that's the truth. But we can't
either of us back out—not when the honor of
the F.A.R. is at stake."

"Mebbe you're right," said the horse. He
sighed, then picked up the flag, and when Mrs.
Wiggins had helped him poke the staff
through his halter so he could carry it upright,
he moved to the center of the line. And Mrs.
Wiggins stepped up beside him and shouted
in her deepest voice: "Forward!"

Mr. Bean took off his hat and stood at attention as the flag of the F.A.R. went by. The
army marched through the barnyard, and
then spread out as it advanced across the
meadows towards the woods. At the duck

pond, Alice and Emma watched it go by.

"Almost seems, sister, as if we ought to be with them," said Alice. "Though what use we'd be in a battle I can't imagine."

"Our Uncle Wesley always said," replied Emma, "that it wasn't strength that counted in warfare, it was courage. And what courage he had, what spirit! He was small, even for a duck, but do you remember the time he spoke so sharply to that tramp cat that was hanging around here?"

"He would have liked us to go along," said Alice. "Sister, I think we should." So the two ducks climbed out of the pond and waddled after the army, a small but very determined rearguard.

Up through the Bean woods the animals went, as quietly as possible, and then spread out by companies along the road while Mrs. Wiggins gave them their orders for the day. Charles would lead the left wing of the army into the Big Woods, keeping well to the left of the Grimby house until he had passed it, when he would swing right to get into contact with the right wing, under Peter, which would have swung around in the same way from the other side. Mrs. Wiggins would give them ten minutes' start, and would then lead the center directly upon the house. Thus the enemy would be completely surrounded, and at a signal from Mrs. Wiggins the army would attack from all sides at once.

Freddy and Randolph were waiting as patiently as they could for the farm animals to put in an appearance. They really didn't have to wait long. Pretty soon the silence was broken by distant sounds, rustlings and snappings, which grew to a continuous crackle and swish, interspersed with occasional crashes as some animal plunged over a fallen log. The noise grew and grew, on both sides of them, and Freddy said:

"I suppose that's their idea of sneaking up on someone. Sounds more like a cyclone coming than anything else. Why can't they be quieter?"

There was a tremendous crash off to the right, and then the voice of Mrs. Wogus: "I declare! I believe I've sprained my right horn. It hit on that tree when I fell. What's the idea of having these trees growing all higgledy-piggledy like this? They ought to be in nice neat rows, then you'd know where you were."

"A swell soldier she makes!" remarked Randolph. "Talk about me not being able to keep my legs from getting mixed up!"

The crashing died down gradually as the animals on the wings took up their positions. But then from behind Freddy came more sounds. The center was advancing directly upon them.

"I'm going up this tree," said Randolph. "No place for me with this mob galloping around. See you later." And he ran quickly up the trunk.

In a minute more Freddy could see Mrs. Wiggins's white nose pushing through the bushes, and to the left of her, and high up, the red, white and blue banner of the F.A.R. jigged along as Hank clambered over stumps and through tangled underbrush. A dozen squirrels came bounding along ahead, and darted up trees to observation posts from which they could watch the activities of the enemy. Then the two dogs came into sight. But only the stealthy movement of a leaf here and there betrayed the presence of the two cats.

Mrs. Wiggins halted her followers behind a screen of trees and surveyed the house. All the animals with her had now seen the gun pointed at them, and the enthusiasm with which they had set out began to evaporate. Freddy ran over to them.

"It's all right," he said. "There's nothing in the gun. I've seen to that. There's no danger."

"Says you!" remarked Jinx. He went over to Mrs. Wiggins. "Listen, General," he said, "if anything happens to me, you kind of look after Minx, won't you? She isn't very bright, but she's all the sister I've got, and—"

"What kind of talk is that on the eve of battle?" demanded the cow severely. "Get in there and fight, cat. Freddy says the gun isn't loaded—"

Several voices were raised. "Oh, he does,

hey?" "Let him walk up and look in it, then."

"Silence in the ranks," said Mrs. Wiggins sternly. She stepped out boldly into full view of the house. "Inside the house, there," she called. "If there's anyone there who has any good reason to offer why we shouldn't come in and tear you to pieces, let him come out under a flag of truce."

There was a scuttling and whispering inside the house, then the door opened a crack and Simon came out, carrying in his mouth a piece of white cloth which looked a good deal like the sleeve of one of Mr. Bean's Sunday shirts.

"Why, as I live and breathe!" he said. "If it isn't my old friend, Mrs. Wiggins!" His upper lip curved back from his long yellow teeth in a sneering smile. "How glad my master, the Ignormus, will be to hear your cheerful moo. Yes, he has been quite peevish today because he had feared to have nothing more tasty for supper than that rather insipid pig there, garnished with carrots and onions, and perhaps a few hard boiled eggs. But a whole cow, now

—that is something like a meal! So you are doubly welcome—both as an old friend, and as something for supper that is big enough for everybody to have a second helping."

"Always the joker, Simon," said Mrs. Wiggins calmly. "But is that all you have to say? Because, if it is, we're coming in."

"My dear Mrs. Wiggins!" said Simon with an oily smirk. "Of *course* you're coming in. A supper invitation from the Ignormus—I tell you, they are not offered to everyone."

"H'm," said Mrs. Wiggins; "with such a soul for hospitality, it does seem odd to me that the Ignormus doesn't come out to greet his guests."

"He'll be out, never fear," replied the rat. "But as you see, he has at first prepared a little reception for you." And he waved a paw towards the window from which the gun protruded.

Mrs. Wiggins didn't like the gun much. Neither, apparently, did her army. For with the exception of Hank, who stood stolidly holding the flag, all of them had become remarkably invisible. If there was going to be a charge, it looked as if she was going to make it all by herself.

Freddy, however, realized what was going on. There was no time to explain about how the gun had been unloaded. He dashed out in front of the army, and directly towards the gun. "Come on, animals!" he shouted. "Down with the Ignormus! Death to Simon and his gang! Oh, go on; shoot your old gun; who's afraid?"

Some of the animals, afterwards—some of them, that is, who were a little envious of Freddy's fine reputation, both as detective and as poet—said that it wasn't very honest of him to act as if he were being a hero, when all the time he knew the gun wasn't loaded. But Freddy knew that it needed a heroic action— at least, one that looked heroic—to get the army to attack the house. He really intended to tell everybody afterwards about the gun, and if he forgot it, and it only got around later through something Randolph said to his old mother, which was repeated to a June bug of her acquaintance, and thus passed on (for the June bug was a terrible gossip) to various insects, and thence to the animals,—well, if he forgot it, I guess we all forget things like that sometimes.

Anyway, his apparent bravery had its effect. The animals jumped up; "Charge!" bellowed Mrs. Wiggins; and Charles on the left and Peter on the right echoed the command. With a crashing of branches and pounding of hoofs and scrabbling of claws the army charged, closing in from all sides on the Grimby house. The din was terrific enough to frighten a dozen Ignormuses, for as the animals charged, they yelled; and since each animal has a different kind of yell, there was a combination of roars and squeaks and screeches and bellows such as has probably never before been brought together at any one time, even in a zoo. And the gun went off with a thunderous Bang!

Chapter 15

Freddy was pretty close to the gun when it went off, and though there were no shot in it, he got a few grains of powder blown into his left shoulder. He was always pretty proud, afterwards, of these scars of honorable warfare, and it was noticed that when he went to the movies he always tried to get a seat on the aisle on the right side of the orchestra, so people would notice them. Of course when he was asked about them, he would never say much, but there was usually some friend with him who would explain to the questioner, and Freddy would look very modest and stern and noble, like an old soldier, to whom such wounds are but trifles.

Well, Freddy wasn't hurt, but there was one shot in the gun that the centipedes had missed, and that buzzed past Freddy and hit a tree and bounced and struck Hank in his off hind leg. It wasn't much of a blow, but Hank had rheumatism in his off hind leg, and there's nothing such a person dislikes so much as to have his attention called to his rheumatism with a sharp blow. Hank was the mildest mannered horse in the state, but now he gave a whinny of rage and bounded forward. With the banner of the F.A.R. fluttering over him, he led the charge right up the porch steps. His feet broke through the rotten floor boards several times, but he plunged on and up to the front door. He put his shoulder against the door and shoved, and as it didn't move, he turned around and let fly a tremendous kick with his two powerful iron-shod hind hoofs. It drove the door off its hinges and halfway down the hall, and the army poured in.

Charles's command, in the meantime, had got in through the cellar door, and after capturing two rats who were on guard there, streamed up the cellar stairs and occupied the kitchen. The right wing, under Peter, had a slower time of it. They found no doors on their side of the house, and the windows were all boarded up. After a short consultation, the two cows stood side by side, close to the house, and Peter got up on their backs, and then the smaller animals: the skunks, and Cecil, the porcupine, and Bill, the goat, climbed up one by one, and Peter, standing on the cows' backs on his hind legs, was just tall enough to pass them up on to the roof, where they at once began clawing away the brittle old shingles. In no time at all they had made holes, through which they dropped into the attic.

It was unfortunate that Peter, though he could get up on the roof, was too big to get through any of the holes between the rafters into the attic. For when the attack on the

Peter got up on their backs.

house had begun, the main body of rats had retreated to the attic, and now the six skunks, the goat and the porcupine found themselves surrounded by a much superior force. The rats, squealing and snarling, advanced upon them. The skunks dove into an empty trunk and managed to pull the lid down so they were safe. Bill backed into a corner, and with sweeps of his long horns kept the attackers at bay. Nevertheless there were so many of them that in time they would probably have pulled him down, if it hadn't been for Cecil. A porcupine almost never fights, but when he does it is always with his back to the enemy. Cecil stood between Bill's forelegs and made occasional backward dashes out at the rats, from which they scattered in alarm. Once, with a quick jerk of his tail, he managed to stick half a dozen quills into the nose of Zeke, who retired whimpering; and another time, a too daring young rat, unfamiliar with the ways of porcupines, bit at him as he came out—and regretted it very bitterly immediately afterward; for a porcupine after all is nothing but a pincushion on four legs, with all the pin points out.

When Peter saw what was going on, he dropped down from the roof and ran around the house and in the front door. The house was full of animals, some of them hunting for rats, others smashing in doors in their search for the Ignormus. They were all so excited and shouting so loud that at first Peter could not make himself heard. But at last he managed to get Hank's attention. The horse was in the kitchen, standing guard over the wash-tubs. Every time a rat was captured, he was dropped into one of the tubs for safe keeping, and Hank had one hoof on the lid, to prevent the prisoners from escaping. He didn't hear very clearly what Peter said to him, and somehow got the idea that it was the Ignormus who was in the attic. But he was still mad clean through about that shot, and if, as he supposed, it was the Ignormus who had fired it at him, he was going to give that Ignormus a beating he wouldn't forget. Hank gave a loud neigh of anger and wheeling, jumped clean over several small animals who were shoving through the doorway and went pounding up the stairs.

He burst into the attic just as Ezra, the largest and toughest of Simon's sons, had darted in under the sweep of Bill's horns and fastened his teeth in the goat's shoulder. Bill reared, and several other rats, avoiding Cecil, charged in, and in another minute they would have pulled Bill down. But with a rush and a clatter of hoofs Hank was on them. He struck at them—right, left, right, left—with his iron front shoes, and with every stroke a rat went crashing into the wall on the other side of the attic. Then with his great front teeth he plucked Ezra from Bill's shoulder, and with a toss of his head, sent the rat sailing out through a hole in the roof. In two minutes there wasn't a rat left in the attic, except those who were lying unconscious against the wall.

So then the skunks came out of the trunk, and the animals dragged the senseless rats downstairs and dropped them into the washtub.

By this time, the excitement in the rest of the house had died down. Every room had been explored, and large parts of the cellar floor had been dug up, to find if the rats had built any secret runways by which they could escape from the house without being seen. But evidently they had felt too safe under the protection of the Ignormus to bother with underground passages. A number had tried to escape through windows and doors, but the squirrel watchers had spotted them, and Jinx and Minx and Georgie had been able to capture them before they got away.

In the pantry off the kitchen the animals found a large store of vegetables, and all the loot that had been stolen from the bank. They also found an old quilt, whose cotton stuffing the rats had used for their false whiskers, and a feather duster which had evidently supplied them with the feathers that they had fastened to their tails to make them look less ratlike. But one thing they didn't find was the Ig-nor-mus.

"It's pretty queer," said Mrs. Wiggins. "If

he's so terrifying and ferocious, my land!—
you'd think he'd come out and fight to protect
his property."

"It's kind of funny, when you come to think
of it," said Mrs. Wogus, "that although we've
heard of him and been afraid of him for years,
there isn't one of us that knows of an animal
that has ever seen him."

"That's why I used to think there wasn't
any such animal," said Freddy. "I just thought
it was a kind of legend that had been built up,
and that he wasn't real at all. But you know
Jinx and I really did see him the other night,
when he came floating down out of the trees
at us like a great white flying squirrel with long
horns. Ugh! That was pretty awful."

"Let's get Simon out and ask him some
questions," said Jinx, and he went over and
rapped on the washtub cover. "Hey, you in
there! We're going to lift the lid a little, and
we want Simon to come out."

So they lifted the lid a little, and a rat came
out. Only it wasn't Simon; it was Ezra.

"We want Simon," said Mrs. Wiggins. "Go back in there and send your father out."

Ezra snickered. "Father isn't there. You thought you were awful smart, didn't you? You thought you'd captured all of us. But you didn't capture father."

"Where is he?" asked Freddy.

"He and the Ignormus went for a walk this morning before you got here," said the rat. " I expect them back any time now. And oh boy! what the Ignormus will do to this gang!"

Some of the animals looked a little nervous at this, but Mrs. Wiggins said: "I think Simon is in there, and if he doesn't come out, I'm going to send Cecil in to look for him."

There was a good deal of squeaking inside the tub when the rats heard this remark, and even Ezra looked rather scared. "Honest, he isn't there," he said. "You just put the lid up and look; I'll make the boys promise not to jump out. But don't send Cecil in."

"It's too bad for you," said the cow, "but you've told too many lies in the past for me to believe you now. Cecil! Where's Cecil?"

The porcupine came up and saluted. "Here, General."

"Go in that tub and see if Simon's there."

"Yes, General." And as the cow lifted the tub cover with one horn, Cecil climbed up and slipped in.

There were a lot of rats in that tub, but they couldn't bite Cecil without getting their noses full of quills. And indeed the more of them there were, the worse it was for them, because it was harder to keep out of the porcupine's way. Cecil looked around thoroughly, and as he wasn't particularly careful to keep from bumping into the prisoners, there was a good deal of shrieking and squeaking before he climbed out again to report that indeed, Simon wasn't there.

The animals were pretty disappointed that they hadn't captured Simon, for he was the ringleader of the whole rat gang. But after all, there wasn't much he could do alone, and it certainly didn't look as if the Ignormus was going to put in an appearance. So leaving

Robert to guard the prisoners, Mrs. Wiggins ordered the army outside, and when they were drawn up in an orderly line before the house, she came to the front door and addressed them.

"Soldiers," she said, "you have fought valiantly and the day is ours."

At this there was prolonged cheering, and Hank, forgetting all about his rheumatism, pranced three times up 'and down in front of the ranks, waving the flag.

"I am proud," Mrs. Wiggins went on, "to be the general of such an army. It is true that our two chief enemies have escaped us. But we have captured their stronghold; the flag of the F.A.R. now waves over the Grimby house—or will, if Hank will stop prancing-around with it and will stick it up on the porch. As for the Ignormus, whatever or wherever he is, I do not think we need to fear him any longer. If he is anywhere in the Big Woods, he heard the Bean legions storming his house, and he plainly did not dare to show himself and to fight.

"However, he may still be lurking in the neighborhood. He and Simon may even now be plotting new crimes. I propose therefore that we take all the stuff here in the house that was stolen from the bank and from Mr. Bean, back down to the farm. We will also take the prisoners and lock them up until we decide what to do with them. Then we will leave a garrison in this house, to defend it if the Ignormus comes back. And I will now call for volunteers to form the garrison."

There wasn't an animal in that army who, twenty-four hours earlier, would have volunteered to spend a night in the Grimby house. But the victory over the rats, and the fact that the Ignormus had apparently been afraid to fight, had made them feel very brave. They stepped forward as one animal.

"Land sakes, you can't all stay," said Mrs. Wiggins. "Guess I'll have to choose. Well, I'll take Peter, because he's a woods animal and very strong, and the two cats, because they can see in the dark, and Charles, because he's licked a rat in fair fight, and Freddy, just in case there's something to detect. That ought to be enough of a garrison. And now, army, get to work and carry the stolen stuff down to the barnyard."

It took the better part of the afternoon to get all the vegetables and oats and nuts and other food supplies down through the woods, and it was nearly dusk when Jinx got back to the Grimby house with a ball of stout twine with which he intended to rope the prisoners together. Jinx was good at tying knots, and as the rats were released one by one from the tub, he tied a loop of cord around each one's middle. Then, with Minx to help him, he started them on the march, like a chain gang, down through the woods.

Freddy was a little doubtful about it. "They can gnaw through those cords and get away, Jinx," he said. "You'd better watch 'em closely."

Jinx laughed. "They'll try it, all right," he said. "Come along, and I'll show you what will happen."

Pretty soon one of the rats began to sneeze.

He sneezed and sneezed, and then another rat began. In a few minutes half the line of prisoners was rolling on the ground, sneezing and coughing and gasping.

"You see?" said Jinx. "That's what happens when they try to gnaw themselves free. I got some red pepper from Mrs. Bean and rubbed it into the whole ball of cord. Come on, boys," he said to the rats. "Get up, and we'll go down to the brook and you can cool your mouths off. Then, if you feel like it, you can try gnawing again."

But the rats had had enough. Except for an occasional sneeze, none of them said anything as they were marched down to the barn and shut up in the box stall, with Cecil left to guard them.

"If any of these lads try anything funny, Cecil," said Jinx, "you just give 'em a little pat with your tail." And the porcupine said he would.

"I guess we'll all have a nice quiet night," he added.

Chapter 16

Freddy had decided that he wouldn't do anything about returning the gun and all the stolen vegetables until next morning. Then he would bring everything out into the barnyard, along with the prisoners, and when Mr. Bean came out after breakfast he would see them and would realize that the rats were the robbers and that Freddy and the other animals had captured them. In that way it wouldn't be necessary to make Mr. Bean feel uncomfortable by saying anything.

But in the meantime Freddy didn't want to be seen around the barnyard. So on the last trip when the rats were taken down, he only went as far as the duck pond, and he waited there for Peter and Charles and the two cats, with whom he was to go back and garrison the Grimby house.

Freddy was pretty pleased with himself. He had found the robbers and recovered the stolen property. It had been a hard case, but he had solved it. "I suppose in my alphabet book, P would stand for pig," he said to himself, and he began making up sentences, all of the words of which began with P. Proud pigs prefer perilous performances. Powerful pig punishes prisoners publicly. Prominent pig proves prowess. "I wish I could use some other letters," he thought. "I can't seem to get everything I want into it." So then he began to make up the verses.

"No better detective than Freddy
  Can be found in the State of New York;
Always calm, always cool, always ready,
  Though a pig, he's by no means just pork.

"Of animals he is the smartest,
  Of pigs he's the brightest by far;
At following clues he's an artist,
  At tracking down crime he's a star."

Freddy had supposed that he was all alone by the duck pond, and he was reciting the verses out loud as he made them up. But he had got this far when he was interrupted by a hoot of laughter, and a deep voice said: "I suppose if nobody else will say those things to you, pig, you have to say them to yourself."

Freddy looked up. It was nearly dark, but in a tree that overhung the pond he could see the shape of a big bird, and he knew it was Old Whibley, the owl. "Oh, it's—it's you," he said with an embarrassed laugh. "Well, I was just sort of—you know—making up anything that came into my head."

Old Whibley didn't say anything.

"Well, what's the matter with that?" demanded Freddy after a minute. "No harm in that, is there?"

"None at all," said the owl. "Who said there was?"

"Well, I thought that you—sort of, well, thought that I—" Freddy stopped, and Old Whibley didn't say anything.

"Oh, gosh," Freddy burst out; "if you're just sitting there thinking I'm vain and conceited, why don't you say so?"

"Why should I?" said the owl. "You know it. I know it. Everybody knows it. No point sitting round and repeating things everybody knows."

"Well," said the pig doubtfully, "maybe I'm a little vain. But that verse, you understand—it was just a sort of joke. Something I was making up as a joke with myself."

"Hoo-o, *hum*," yawned Old Whibley.

"But don't you think I'm a good detective?" asked Freddy.

"Good enough," said the owl. "Anyway, if you're satisfied, who am I to complain?"

"Goodness," said Freddy. "I must say it's hard enough to get anything out of you. I should think you could give an opinion when you're asked for it."

"You haven't been asking for my opinion," said the owl. "You've been trying to get me to say how grand and wonderful you are. I don't think you're so grand. Not when you sit around singing songs of praise to yourself, and leaving your work half done."

"I don't see how you can say that," said Freddy. "We captured the robbers and got back all the stolen goods."

"You haven't captured the head robber, Simon. And it seems to me there was some big boast of yours how you were going to capture the Ignormus and nail his hide to the barn door. I was up past the barn a minute ago, and there wasn't any hide there then."

There was one nice thing about Freddy: he was always willing to acknowledge it when he was wrong. At least he was willing to after a while. Usually there had to be an argument first.

But now there wasn't anything to argue about. "Well," he said; "well—maybe you're right. I guess I was so pleased at getting all the things back, and specially the gun, that I sort of forgot about the rest of it." He thought a minute. "Yes, you're right. My job isn't finished. I talked pretty big, didn't I? Well, it's up to me. I guess I won't wait for the rest of the garrison. I'll go up myself, and if I can find the Ignormus, I'll have it out with him."

He waited a minute, then as Old Whibley didn't say anything, he looked up into the tree. But the owl wasn't there.

"Well, I'll be darned!" said Freddy. "He might have given me a *little* praise for *that.* After all, I'm risking my life." He hesitated a minute. He didn't hear anything to show that his friends were coming. "I suppose that owl is around here, watching, somewhere. I suppose I'll *have* to go now." And he started slowly up through the woods.

It was hard going in the dark, and when he got to the road Freddy sat down to rest. "Whew!" he said out loud. "Guess I'll have to rest a minute." He said this because he thought Old Whibley might still be watching him, and he didn't want the owl to think he was afraid. But no sound came from the tall trees on either side of the road, and after resting a minute that was long enough to have several hundred seconds in it, he got up and said in a bold, loud voice: "Well, now for the Ignormus!"

He was standing just about where he and Jinx had been when that terrifying white shape had plunged down towards them from the treetops, and as he started across the road towards the darkness of the Big Woods he glanced fearfully up—and gave a squeal of sheer terror. For there it was again, floating down upon him: a great white body as big as Mrs. Wiggins and Mrs. Wurzburger and Mrs. Wogus rolled into one, with a huge horned head that waggled menacingly.

Freddy said afterward that his squeal was a squeal of defiance, and he also said that he stood his ground, prepared to do or die—willing—nay, eager—to have it out with this

monster who for so many years had terrorized
the countryside. I think the real reason he
didn't run was that he was too scared. He
wanted to get away from that place as quickly
as possible. But his legs either didn't understand what he wanted, or else they were too
scared themselves to hold him up. For they
collapsed under him, and the great white creature floated down and enveloped him.

I don't think Freddy really fainted away, but
it was certainly several seconds before he
realized that he was struggling to get out from
under what seemed to be heavy folds of cloth.
He kicked and scrabbled in a panic, and at last
wrestled his way out into the open air, and
then turned to see what he had been wrestling
with. It was a sheet—plainly one of the sheets
that had been stolen from Mrs. Bean's clothes-
line. In each knotted corner of the sheet was
a stone, and to one end of it had been fastened
the tail of one of Mr. Bean's Sunday shirts.

"Oh, my goodness!" exclaimed the pig.
"The Ignormus! *This* is the Ignormus! They
carried it up into the treetops and let it float

"Who's that you've got there?" Freddy asked.

down on us like a parachute. And the shirt was the head, with the arms for horns. Well, what do you know about that for a trick!"

He became aware, then, of a terrified squeaking that had been going on for some time up in the tree from which the Ignormus had been launched upon him. And as he looked up, Old Whibley came soaring down on his silent wings and lit on a bough just over his head. He seemed to have something in his powerful beak,—something that squeaked and wriggled and twisted in a vain effort to escape, and as Freddy looked, the owl shifted the writhing animal to one claw and said: "Thought I'd come along to see how you made out. Well, you caught your Ignormus."

"Who's that you've got there?" Freddy asked. "Looks like Simon."

"Probably is," said Old Whibley. "Means nothing to me. One rat's the same as any other rat, far as I'm concerned. None of 'em any good. Saw him drop that sheet out of a tree so I grabbed him."

"You mean he was up in the tree? I never knew rats could climb trees."

"They can't climb smooth trees. But with all the little branches on these spruce trees, it's easy enough. You want him?"

"I want to ask him some questions," said Freddy.

"I won't answer," squeaked Simon. "I won't say a word. And you wait till the Ignormus hears about this; you just wait—"

"Oh, keep still about your old Ignormus," interrupted Freddy. "There never was any Ignormus, and you know it as well as I do."

A twig snapped, and a moment later Peter and the two cats and Charles came out into the road

"Oh, there you are, Freddy," said Jinx. "We were looking for you. What on earth's this?" And he walked over to the sheet.

"Ha!" exclaimed Freddy. "You know what that is? It's the Ignormus's hide, that's what it is. And I'm going to take it down and nail it to the barn door, as I said I would."

"I can't see much of anything in the dark here," said Peter, "but it looks to me like an old sheet."

So Freddy explained. "It was a trick of the rats'," he said. "They got it up in the tree somehow and then when they wanted the Ignormus to appear, they dropped it, and these stones in the corners made it float down like a parachute."

"Well, what do you know!" said Jinx. "You know, Freddy, that time before when it dropped down on us, I thought there was something funny about it. That's why I wasn't as scared as you were—"

"Weren't scared, eh, cat?" interrupted Old Whibley. "Listen, I was over on the Flats that night, and I heard you yell, way over there. If there was ever a scareder cat I never heard him."

Jinx peered up into the branches overhead. "Oh, is that you, Whibley? Didn't see you. Well, of course I yelled. I was—well, startled. But scared! Pooh! I hope I don't scare that easy."

"You can give up that hope right now," replied the owl. "I never knew an easier scared cat. Remember that night when the mouse jumped out at you in Witherspoon's barn? You did the two miles home in—"

"Please, please," interrupted Jinx. "Let's not go into past history. After all, if this really is the Ignormus, it's pretty big news."

"When I was in South Africa," said Minx, "there was an elephant who had learned to fly. He'd been taking flying lessons from an ostrich, and—"

"Ostriches can't fly," said Jinx. "How could your elephant learn to fly by taking lessons from somebody that can't fly?"

"This ostrich *could* fly," said Minx. "Because he had taken lessons from an eagle. And so the elephant learned how, and—"

"Listen, sis," interrupted Jinx impatiently; "just forget about this elephant friend of yours, will you? We want to find out about this Ignormus."

"But I *want* to tell you about him," insisted Minx. "His name was—"

"Sure, 'twas Murphy, was it not?" said Freddy, suddenly coming close to Minx and speaking with the terrible Irish accent he had used when he had stopped her telling stories before. "Indeed and I remimber him well."

"No, it was *not*," said Minx crossly. "And if you're going to do that again, I won't tell you about him."

"Sure an' all, since I know all about him, why should you?" said Freddy. And Minx walked away, switching her tail angrily.

"I was just trying to get Simon to tell us a few things when you came, Jinx—" said Freddy. "But he didn't seem to want to. Suppose you could make him? You know, by tickling him as you did last time?"

"Sure, hand him over to me, Whibley," said the cat. "You know, I just love tickling that rat. It's the funny noises he makes. It's sort of like that old Mr. Mackintosh, in Centerboro, when he plays on the bagpipes. Come here, rat; let's see if I can't get a better tune out of you than I did last time."

The owl dropped the rat to the ground, and

the cat pounced on him. "What'll it be, Simon?" he said. "Something patriotic?"

"I'll talk," said the rat sullenly. "If you just won't tickle me. I can't stand that."

So the others gathered around, and Simon told them how when he and his family had been driven from the farm, they had wandered about, leading a sort of gipsy life, stealing food from farmers along the road, and sleeping in barns and deserted houses. But it was a dangerous life, for no other animals trust rats, and dogs and cats chased them whenever they saw them. So they were thinking about some place where they could settle down in safety when Simon thought of the Grimby house. Of course they had all heard about the Ignormus, and some of them were afraid, but Simon had several times been obliged to take refuge in the Big Woods when chased by the Bean dogs, and he had seen nothing of any such monster. He didn't believe in him. "We'll go back," he had said, "and explore the Big Woods. If we find there isn't any Ignormus there—and I'm pretty sure

there isn't—we'll settle down in the old Grimby house. Nobody will molest us there, or
even know we're there, and we can raid the
Bean farm as much as we want to, and nobody
will ever know, because no animal dares to
enter the Big Woods."

So the rats had done just that. And if Freddy
hadn't got so curious about the Ignormus, and
if he hadn't himself begun to doubt the exist-
ence of any such animal, they might have lived
there very comfortably. For by threatening
letters, signed by the Ignormus, and by the
trick of the parachute-sheet, and in other
ways, they had built up the legend of the Ignormus and spread a belief in him and a terror of him among the animals, until all those
on the Bean farm,—who really hadn't thought
much about him for a long time—began to be
really afraid even to live near the Big Woods.

"Well," said Old Whibley, when Simon
had finished, "it all goes to show."

"Show what?" Jinx asked.

"Work it out for yourself," said the owl,
and flew away.

"Well, he's a big help," said Jinx. "What'll we do with Simon, Freddy?"

"Have to decide that later. Take him down and lock him up, now. And there's no use going up to garrison the Grimby house." He began rolling up the sheet. "I'm going to take this down with me. Give me a hand, Charles."

The next morning Mr. Bean was sitting at the table having breakfast. He had just had fourteen buckwheat pancakes and three cups of coffee and was finishing a piece of apple pie when he heard a sound of hammering down by the barn.

"Well, what *now?*" he exclaimed, and it shows how surprised he was that he got up and went out on the porch, for Mrs. Bean had just put six more buckwheat cakes on his plate and was going in the pantry to get some doughnuts. Mr. Bean always liked to top off his breakfast with five or six doughnuts.

Freddy was tacking something up on the barn door.

"What on earth!" exclaimed Mrs. Bean, who had come out behind her husband.

"Why, that's one of my sheets that was stolen."

"And one of my Sunday shirts," said Mr. Bean.

Freddy disappeared into the barn, and came running out in a minute, dragging the shotgun. And behind him came a whole crowd of small animals carrying the vegetables —some of them looking pretty wilted—which had been stolen from the garden. And last came the chain gang of rats, guarded by the cats.

"Well, I'll be hornswoggled!" exclaimed Mr. Bean, and this was pretty strong language for him, particularly so early in the morning.

Jinx led the rats right up to the porch steps, and lined them up in front of the Beans.

"Lie down on your backs and confess your crimes," he commanded.

After a good deal of getting tangled up in the cord, and several bad fits of sneezing, the rats managed to get on their backs with their legs in the air. All, that is, except Simon, who said with a snarl: "I won't do it."

"Ho!" said Jinx with a grin. "Being the

head rat, I suppose you've got too much dignity, hey? Well, I guess I can tickle some of that dignity out of you." And he crouched, and crept slowly toward Simon.

The rat pretended not to pay any attention at first, but as Jinx came closer and closer he began to tremble, and gave a nervous giggle, and then he rolled over on his back. "All right, all right," he said angrily. "I can't stand that tickling."

"That's better," said the cat. "Now, boys, repeat what you have to say to Mr. Bean."

So the rats, in unison, repeated the words Jinx had spent the last hour in teaching them. "Oh, Mr. Bean, we are the thieves who stole your oats. We stole your gun from Freddy. We stole your washing off the line. We robbed the vaults of the First Animal Bank. We pretended that we were the Ignormus, who lives in the Big Woods, and we frightened all the animals and made them steal the vegetables from your garden."

The rest of the rats stopped, but Simon went on: "And if you'll forgive us and let us go, we promise not to do it any more."

"Hey, hey!" protested Jinx. "That wasn't what I told you to say. And it isn't true, either. We've let you go twice before, rats, and each time you've come back and done something worse. No sir, this time Mr. Bean is going to decide what is to be done with you."

There was silence for a little while, and then Mr. Bean turned to Mrs. Bean. "Well, Mrs. B.," he said, "what'll we do with the pesky critters? Rats are no good. They're the one animal you can't trust. Except maybe tigers. But I never had any experience of tigers, so I don't know. Well, what'll we do? Shoot 'em?"

Mrs. Bean smiled and shook her head.

"Drown 'em?" said Mr. Bean.

She shook her head again.

Mr. Bean thought for quite a while, then he said: "Hang 'em up by their tails?"

"Mercy, no!" exclaimed Mrs. Bean.

So then Mr. Bean shook *his* head. "I come to the end of my ideas," he said. "I guess you'll have to decide, Mrs. B."

So then Mrs. Bean thought for a while. And at last she said: "I don't like rats any better than you do, Mr. B. But maybe it isn't their fault that they're bad. Maybe they didn't have the right kind of bringing up. And, maybe, too, it isn't easy for them to be good, even if they want to. I mean that when everybody suspects them, and all the cats and dogs chase them, it's hard for them to get a living, and they almost have to steal to get enough to eat. That's what I think, Mr. B. And so I'd like to try something else. I'd like to give them that old barn up in the back pasture to live in. You don't use it for anything. And I'd like to promise them three square meals a day. Freddy could take charge of seeing to that. I think if they have a place to live, and plenty to eat, like the other farm animals, they'll behave like the other animals. How about it, Mr. B.?"

"It does credit to your kind heart, Mrs. B.," replied Mr. Bean. "Though in my opinion, rats are rats, and always will be. But we'll try it. Turn 'em loose, Jinx."

Some, indeed most, of the younger rats

were so affected by Mrs. Bean's kindness that they burst into tears. But Simon merely sneered, and when he was set free, he said to Mrs. Bean: "My family seem inclined to accept your hospitality, ma'am, and I have nothing to say against it. Try it if you like. But they've been brought up to be thieves, and thieves they'll always be, as you'll find out. Oh, they'll behave well enough for a time, I've no doubt. But as for me, I'm too old to change. For me, it's the open road, where I can do as I please, and not be bound by rules that are laid down for me by somebody else. So good day to you, ma'am." And he turned and started towards the gate.

Jinx started after him, but Mrs. Bean called the cat back. "Let him go," she said. "I'm sure he won't bother us any more."

Simon turned. "Thank you, ma'am," he said. "And I'll tell you this: I've had the first kind word from you today that I've had from any animal or human since the day I was born. Oh, I don't want kind words, and I don't deserve 'em. But because you've given me them, I'll promise you this: that from now on I'll leave the Bean farm alone." And he turned and walked out of the gate, and off up the road.

When Jinx had released the rats, and they had scurried off to their new home, Mrs. Bean said: "Well, I think this calls for a party. Animals, you're all invited to a party in the front parlor at five this afternoon. And then you can tell us about your experiences catching the robbers. If Mr. B. doesn't mind," she added, looking at her husband.

"Can't find out how they did it unless I hear 'em talk," he said. "So I'll have to put up with it for once." And he picked up his gun and went in the house to finish his breakfast.

But Freddy went up to Mrs. Bean. "I'd like to ask some friends of mine to the party, if it's all right. They helped me a lot on this case."

"Why, ask anyone you've a mind to," said Mrs. Bean.

"Well," said Freddy, "I thought maybe you

wouldn't like to have them. One's a frog, and one's a beetle, and then there's a centipede and his—"

"A centipede!" she exclaimed. "Oh dear, Freddy, I don't know about centipedes. I'm afraid Mr. Bean might object. I'm afraid he'd think maybe a centipede wouldn't quite know how to behave at a party. Would I have to shake hands with him?" she inquired doubtfully.

"Oh no, ma'am," said the pig. "Jeffrey's kind of a rough diamond, if you know what I mean. I guess you'd only embarrass him if you shook hands with him."

"I'm sure it would embarrass me," said Mrs. Bean.

"I could bring them in a bottle," said Freddy. "I think they'd feel better that way, with Charles and Henrietta around. But I'm sure they'd like to come, and see the inside of the house, with the new wallpaper and all. They could see all right through the bottle if I washed it first."

So Mrs. Bean consented rather doubtfully,

and Freddy went off to admire the sheet he
had tacked up on the barn door.

Randolph was walking up the sheet when
he got there.

"Hi, Freddy," said the beetle. "I guess you
kind of forgot me up there in the Big Woods.
After I went up that tree, before the attack.
It's all right. I got a ride down on one of the
squirrels. Boy, this Ignormus hide is some
hide, eh?"

"I said I'd get it and nail it to the barn door,
and I did," said the pig.

"Good job," said Randolph. "And yet—"

"Yet what?" said Freddy sharply.

"Don't like to seem to criticize," said Randolph. "But after all. There wasn't any Ignormus, was there?"

"Well, I don't know," said Freddy. "There
was and there wasn't, if you know what I
mean. Plenty of animals were scared of him.
Scareder than they'd been of a herd of wild al-
ligators. Seems to me that if you believed in
the Ignormus, why then as far as you were concerned, there *was* an Ignormus. And he was

just as terrible and horrible and ferocious as you thought he was. And it was just as brave of all those animals to go into the Big Woods to attack him, as it would have been if he'd really been there."

"I see what you mean," said the beetle. "The trick is, not to believe in anything awful. Then you're not scared of it. Yes. Well, take beetles. Nobody ever bothers a beetle. A beetle's life is just one long picnic. Or should be. Then why do beetles hide under stones, and duck out of sight when they see a shadow? I'll tell you. They're born scared. Scared of things they can't see. Scared of things there really aren't any of. Like Ignormuses. If you could find one beetle that wasn't really scared of anything he couldn't see, that beetle would be a king."

"You've done a lot of thinking about life, I guess," said Freddy respectfully.

"Did a lot while I was up that tree," said Randolph. "Saw how the things we're most scared of don't exist. Thing to do is, walk right up to them and say: 'Mister, you're just an

Ignormus. You aren't there. Get out of my way.' And then, sure enough, they disappear like a puff of smoke."

"You're right," said Freddy. "The Ignormus had every animal on this farm scared for years. And what was he? Nothing. My goodness, I'm not ever going to be scared of anything again."

At this moment, Jinx, who had come up stealthily behind the pig, gave a loud screech. Freddy went straight up in the air, and then, with a terrified squeal, bolted into the barn.

The cat grinned. "There you are," he said. "Not going to be scared of anything again, hey? And look at him."

"Sure," said Randolph. "Guess we can't help it. Guess we'll all of us always be scared by things that don't really amount to much."

"Meaning me?" said the cat sharply.

"If you don't amount to much, you ought to know it better than I do," said Randolph. Then, as the cat stared ferociously at him, he ducked into a crack in the door.

"Ha," said Jinx. *"He* should talk about be-

ing scared! *Yow!* " he yelled. "What was *that*?"
For something long and snaky had suddenly
dropped across his back, and in three jumps
he was up on the fence across the barnyard.

Freddy, who had thrown the old piece of
rope down from the door to the loft, which
was above the big barn door, stuck his head
out.

"That makes us all even, cat," he called.

Jinx started to get mad, then suddenly he
laughed.

"Guess you and your bug friend are right,"
he said. "There's always something to scare
us, and usually it turns out to be nothing at all.
Ignormuses, or pieces of rope, or whatever it
is."

"Yes," said Freddy. "We've got one Ignormus's hide nailed up, but there'll always be
others. Little ones or big ones."

"There'll always be Ignormuses," said the
cat. And personally I think it was the wisest
thing he, or any other cat, is ever likely to say.